HALF SICK OF SHADOWS

RICHARD ABBOTT

ISBN: 978-0993-1684-9-9 (soft cover)
ISBN: 978-0993-1684-8-2 (ebook format)

Matteh Publications

Contact:
Web: http://mattehpublications.datascenesdev.com/
Email: matteh@datascenesdev.com

HALF SICK OF SHADOWS

For Roselyn, for family

Contents

Also by the Author

Science Fiction
Novels:
> Far from the Spaceports
> Timing

Historical Fiction
Novels:
> In a Milk and Honeyed Land
> Scenes from a Life
> The Flame Before Us

Short stories:
> The Lady of the Lions
> The Man in the Cistern

Cover information

Cover artwork © Copyright Mary Abbott

Original Matteh Publications logo drawn by Jackie Morgan.

Birth

THE LADY AWOKE. The courtyard was dark, and the kindly darkness was all around her. Everything was new. She was among leaves, leaves and flowers, and she was nourished with no need to move.

There was a remembrance of light, of grand movements in a greater space, but she could make no sense of it. She ate, and she slept, and she changed.

In the next room, across from her sleeping form, the Mirror waited for her to progress beyond childish things. It was dormant, while the lady lay as an infant.

Outside, the courtyard walls waited for warmth, grey in the midst of the glacial land. They kept the lady's flower garden warm, delicate, safe from all that was outside. Four towers faced the compass quadrants, sturdy and strong. During her sleep, an age of ice withdrew, and the land lifted. It began to breathe again as the weight retreated northwards.

Great furry beasts strayed nearby, teeth and tusks as white as the blanketed land. They spared no glance for the walls and the towers of the courtyard as they browsed by, their footfalls fading with a breath of new snow.

Nobody was watching.

Instar 1

THE LADY WOKE, larger than she had been, more aware of what was around. She wriggled from the nest which had held her, found a cache of tender leaves, and started to feast herself.

Then she looked around, becoming interested in the space that arched above her, the sights and scents of her garden. The memory of her origins had slipped away, but something about the vaulting room was familiar. If anything was home, this was, though some hidden part of her knew there had to be more.

Her waking mind provoked resonance in the Mirror. It warmed to life, images starting to stir in its grey depths. She went towards it, fascinated by the play of light and colour. The pattern settled to something more stable: blue above and green below, with waving fronds clear against the background. But it was a sludgy, begrudging green, which still remembered bitter winters and late springs. It was quite unlike the rich verdancy she enjoyed within the confines of her courtyard and towers.

She chewed idly on another leaf, watching the shapes move. There was a dais facing the Mirror, with a plinth on it, and a little stick projecting from that. She heaved herself up on the dais. The stick was at just the right height for one of her hands, and she took hold of it, not knowing what it was for.

The Mirror hummed at her, a gentle note that made her happy. The edges glowed, and a little circle of light appeared. She stared at it, but nothing else happened. She ate the rest of her leaf, placidly watching the blue and green shapes combine. Every so often white puffs drifted across the blue.

And then something brown came by, brown and purposeful, moving on four legs which seemed too thin to hold its weight. It moved in quick steps which spoke of anxiety. A smaller copy moved in its shadow, and others like it were at a distance. They were moving together across the land.

She leaned forward, curious about the changes, and the circle of light slid across the surface to outline the brown shape. The stick buzzed in her hand. She looked at it, puzzled, and squeezed it. A happy sound filled the room and the bright circle flashed once. It was fun.

A little shining bubble drifted up from the circle towards the top of the Mirror. It was full of little gleaming shapes, and when it reached the rim it burst in a fizz of sound and sparkle. That was even more fun.

She thought about it as she sucked the sap from the veins of another leaf. The bright ring was still outlining the original brown thing. She squeezed it again. Nothing happened. She frowned at it, but nothing happened. Struck by a thought, she angled the stick down, and it slid neatly over the smaller shape. This time the squeeze worked, and another bubble rose and burst for her. So: it only worked once for any one thing.

She moved the circle over the brown shapes in turn and squeezed, not waiting for each to finish. Then she sat back and enjoyed the play of brightness and melody, as it showered the expanse in front of her. She watched for a while as the things moved out of the Mirror's view. There was nothing to do now. It had been a good game, but now she was bored.

And in any case, she was tired. She ate, and she slept, and she changed.

The Mirror sent its own signals, chasing after those that she had captured. Then it waited again, and monitored her sleeping body as the years passed.

Outside, the chill of centuries of snow was melting rapidly, and trees were creeping across the lands. Up on the ridge, they were scrubby, shallow-rooted, but here in the valley, they grasped deep and reached high beside the winding river.

Herds of animals grazed the woodland glades, trailing further north each generation as the memories of ice receded. Sometimes a group would come up to the grey stone walls, scenting some trace of the garden of flowers they held. But there was no archway to be found, no entrance to the delights within, and they moved on by.

And although predators followed the herds, they too were just beasts. The Mirror watched a flying creature here, a running one there, observing the signs of intelligence among them. They were interesting, and worth recording, but they did not quite match what it was expecting. It was looking for something quite specific, and willing to wait. Meanwhile, it had the lady to nurture.

Instar 2

THE LADY WOKE AGAIN. She was no larger in body this time than she had been before, but her mind had considerably expanded. She had a clear sense that she had been awakened deliberately, as though to some schedule, but she could not tell why.

As she snacked on bundles of mixed leaves she worked her way over to the Mirror. The dais had changed while she slept. There was a couch on it now, shaped to fit her own form. In place of the original single stick there were two, and they ended in little clusters of buttons. She wriggled onto the couch, and the sticks were at just the right place for her front limbs. She grasped them, and found that the buttons were perfectly placed as well. While she had been sleeping, all this had been reshaped for her.

The Mirror held a sharper, brighter image now, unless it was her own eyes which had changed. She looked out at the view. The rolling ridge of hills in the distance was clothed with plants, and the upper slopes were alive with flowers, dotted like stars, young and yellow among the scattered shrubs. The new leaves were still springing from their buds. The valley below was more rounded, its former glacial lines softened by the river running through it. It was a good land.

By way of experiment she waggled the two control sticks, one at a time. The left hand one moved the view, side to side, up and down. She entertained herself for a while spinning the frame round and round, seeing how fast she could make it go before the shapes blurred with motion. The one to her right zoomed the Mirror's view in and out. She took it in close to see a single leaf as it fluttered idly in the breeze, then lifted back to absorb the whole panorama again.

She looked around her chamber then. There was no shortage of leaves inside the four grey walls, nor of flowers, but they were never stirred by random puffs and gusts of wind. Only the steady pulse of mechanical fans pushed past them, ensuring they were kept moist and pollinated. She stopped briefly, trying to think back to when the word pollination had entered her mind. Surely it was while she slept. But although the word was there, the meaning was not; it was just a thing that happened to plants.

Unconcerned by her ignorance, she looked back out through the Mirror again. Opposite the broad bend of the river by which her towers were built, there were traces of movement, indistinct brown amongst the green. She pushed the right-hand lever forwards, until the shapes of animals popped into focus. Remembering last time, she squeezed the stick to get her reward of light and sound. The Mirror made a disappointed sound. Nothing happened. The game must change each time, she thought.

She looked at the buttons, pushed at the largest one, and a noose of light appeared on the Mirror's surface. She played at moving it around, finding out how combinations of pushes and movements changed its shape. Finally, she circled the lead animal and pressed the largest button again. There was a happy sound, and sparkles rippled around the Mirror's frame. She nodded to herself, pleased. Older than before, she was no longer so impressionable as to imagine that the surface was everything, but it felt good to have worked it out.

"I wonder what they are?"

It was the first time she had spoken, and she imagined her voice sounded rough, tuneless. Then, feeling awkward at disturbing the wall of silence, she squirmed on her couch and looked around. Nobody was there. It puzzled her. Why would she have the ability to speak, if there was nobody to listen? She called out, three times over, louder each time until she was shouting.

"What are they?"

Only empty echoes answered.

Turning back to the Mirror, she saw that a little circling bubble had appeared over the head of the first animal. It had not been there before. She snagged it with the noose, and a rush of knowledge came to her.

They were herd animals, plant eaters like herself but able to tear through coarse vegetable matter of a kind she could not stomach. In a passing moment, she learned how much land the group would need for foraging, the mix of males, females, and young, and the rate at which they were declining as the climate changed.

She had closed her eyes to absorb the details, and when she looked up again the bubble had gone. She nodded. The bubble was not really outside, not in the way that the beasts were. It had only ever been on the Mirror.

"It was only ever a shadow."

Nobody answered her call.

She span the view round so that she could see the river valley again, and her gaze was caught by a thin lazy spiral rising up from a grassy hillock on the other bank. It curled and wove itself into shapes which hovered on the verge of making sense. This time she whispered.

"I wonder what that is."

Another bubble appeared on the screen, and she snagged it, ready this time for the sensation of understanding filling her thoughts. It was smoke, a by-product of making heat or light, which her own environment did not need. The smoke arose from wood as it changed from living thing to ash. She understood that the wood itself would be too tough to eat, even for the herd animals she had seen. It would have to be processed in a different way.

"Can they eat this smoke?"

She waited, but nothing happened. It was still a game, then. Some things she would be told, and others she must learn for herself. The Mirror would not instruct her about everything.

She fiddled with the two sticks again, and the Mirror's view rushed out to meet her. At the bottom of the plume of smoke, the wood was being consumed by flickering red tongues. That was fire, she learned, consuming the wood, and the fuel itself came from branches of the nearby trees after they had dried for a season.

One of the furry animals lay limply nearby, its body fluids captured in a bowl. One of its legs was suspended on a frame above the fire. It all made no sense, until she realised that the Mirror was telling her about nourishment. Even then, it was hard to comprehend.

"Nourishing who? And why not just be nourished on the tender parts of the plants?"

There was no answer. She brought the view back a little, and saw two other creatures, sitting on stones near the fire. One of them was considerably larger than the other. Most likely she was looking at an adult and a juvenile. They were a different shape altogether, more upright, with much less body fur. They made up for the lack of natural covering by draping themselves with things they had made. They had tools, and projected confidence rather than anxiety. As she watched, the larger one stirred the fire so that sparks arose with the smoke, turning the roasting leg to heat evenly.

Their mouths were moving – their teeth were quite unlike those of the herd animals – and seeing the interplay between them she realised, with a sudden thrill, that they were speaking. But she could hear nothing.

"I want to hear them. Mirror, do you understand me? I want to hear the sounds they make."

Nothing happened. She stared at them, trying to guess what their words might mean. Inside her four walls was a great silence. She zoomed right in to one of the faces, and then left the dais to press herself close to the Mirror. But try as she might, she could hear no trace of sound.

Frustrated, she moved the view back again. Like the herd animals, they had only four limbs, and she allowed herself a look of measuring pride down the length of her body. Four would scarcely be enough to balance, let alone move with assurance. Then one of the pair turned to look off to one side, and following the glance she saw three others approaching. One was adult, though with more curves than either of the first two individuals. The next was shorter, about half the size, and the last was so small it had to be held.

It was not the possibility of group which entranced her at first, though, but the fact that all of them moved on just two legs. The balance looked precarious, as though they were continually on the verge of falling as they moved. But, she acknowledged generously, having their whole upper body free to carry out all kinds of tasks as they moved about was convenient.

She stared at them for a long time, fascinated by their otherness. Surely, they were something quite alien. But then, with the internal assurance of fact that came from the Mirror, she knew that one day, she would look not unlike these creatures.

It was a disturbing thought, and improbable, given their current appearance. The Mirror's rim chimed softly at her, and she absently tagged each of the five with the noose of light. It hardly took any thought now, and her attention remained fixed on them. After a while the largest one took the animal's leg from above the fire, chewed at it, and passed it around the circle. An uneasy thrill passed through her body. They nourished themselves like this, allowing the herd beasts to change plant matter into food for them, instead of taking it in directly.

"Do others eat in this way? Or is it just them?"

A quick flow of images passed across her mind, showing different habits of food. Hunters and hunted, predator and prey, mild and savage: the creatures she was watching were somewhere in the middle of that spectrum. It was an uncomfortable, visceral vision. She shook her head to clear it, and went back to watching the group.

They were easy with each other, enjoying each other's company. The smallest one took no meat, but clung to the curvy one and suckled for a time. She smiled, at last feeling something in common, and shared the meal with them by sucking at the veins of a leaf.

The sky slowly drained of colour, and after a time they stood and ambled in their ungainly off-balance stride over to some trees. There was a wooden structure under the grey branches, she saw, and one after another they went in. The largest one stayed outside longest, looking around as though trying to find something.

Suddenly it looked straight across the valley towards her walls and towers, as though it knew of her presence, as though its gaze could penetrate back through the Mirror. It called something, and beckoned, and the curvy one came out to join him, following the larger one's gaze and pointing arm. They stared together across the valley at her, spoke together, nodded together.

All at once the lady felt the pressure of them watching. She flinched away, in case some alien sight could pierce her, but the moment passed, and she was left alone again. Surely the couple could not be aware of her? But if there could be awareness, perhaps there could be converse.

"Can I talk with them? I will talk with them. I want to meet them. Make it so I can meet them, Mirror."

There was no answer, except for the deep certainty that it could not happen. There was a block in her mind around the idea, a solemn awareness that to meet would be perilous. But at the same moment, she was aware of a deep desire for the creatures to see her, to know her.

She spent days watching the group, and their way of life. She was fascinated by their ambulation, and in the privacy of her chamber tried to imitate it. But she was not built for that, and she knew she looked foolish. Her natural movement was horizontal, flowing, sinuous, and she could not master a vertical stance.

Sometimes they met with others of their kind, who walked over to be with them in the cool of the evening from their own wooden huts. But in the lady's mind, these others were only visitors, and her first acquaintances were her real family. Breaths of wind tickled the leaves and shaped the fire's smoke into wreaths and coils.

She diligently tagged everything else in view, living and non-living, static and moving alike, and the Mirror taught her how to group similar items together. She no longer saw things as entirely separate, but as sets and collections. She played at organising what she watched in different ways according to her mood. One day it would be by size, another day by colour, another by speed of movement.

But always she went back to watching the family group. Since the Mirror gave her sight, but not sound, she made up names as she pleased. She set her viewing position up alongside them, as though she was sharing their provisions and their family life. When their lips moved in speech, she would chatter alongside them, pretending that each could hear the other.

She tried to imitate the way the adults related to each other and their offspring. Generally, it was easy-going, casual, teasing. They laughed often, except once when the largest one was irate over some careless breakage. The lady shrank away from the force of emotion, then slowly returned to her place in the circle as the group reconciled and settled together again.

She knew that they were aware of her, as a hovering presence on the borderland between the firelight and the flickering shadows. The younger ones took no more notice of her than they did of the leaves stirring in the wind. The two adults would sometimes pause their own communications and turn towards her, as though seeking opinion or resolution. She had no idea what they wanted her to say, but it fed her soul to be included.

All five were a constant study for her. Of them all, she found the smallest one the most immediately fascinating. It depended entirely on the others for everything. It needed to be carried, and so far as she could tell, the more curved of the adults supplied all of its food, from somewhere inside itself.

For a week, she felt superior to them in every way, until a meal time one day. As usual, she delayed eating so she could play at sharing the occasion with them. When the infant began suckling, she picked up the best of the leaves she had selected. Then she stopped and stared at it. She had done as little to deserve this food as the child out there. She relied entirely on the Mirror's provision.

"Mirror, I am just like that infant."

The Mirror said nothing. She put the leaf down again. The meal was spoiled for her. She threw all the leaves on the floor and stamped on them, her little feet bruising the veins and spilling the sap. Her voice was high pitched, petulant.

"I want to go to them. You have to let me go out there."

There was no reply. Like before, there was only a cold refusal. It was not right.

She stormed out of the room, going into the courtyard with its high walls. She savoured the scent of exotic flowers, even as she roamed around the perimeter to find a way out. But she found none. She picked a blossom from her favourite shrub and wriggled back in to the Mirror's room.

The mess of leaf was gone: somehow it had been cleaned away while she had been out of the room. She put the bloom onto the dais and pointed out at the moving shadows on the Mirror's surface. They had finished eating now, and two of the creatures were busy fashioning some implement from a dark shard of stone.

"Why are there no flowers like this outside? There should be. That child would like them. I want to give them one of my flowers."

She paused.

"And I want somebody to hold me like the curvy one holds the infant when it suckles."

There was no answer. She refused to tag anything for two whole days. She tried to deny herself food, but hunger soon defeated her. She talked endlessly to the creatures as they went about their lives, and sometimes, she was sure, they responded to her.

"I will give you one of my flowers some day."

But, as the next day dawned, she found herself vastly hungry. She could not keep herself from the piles of fresh leaves, the little bowls of glistening sap. All her thoughts were consumed by the craving to eat. And drowsiness followed on the heels of the satisfaction of food.

All through that day she struggled to keep attentive to her family, and most especially the adults. She stared at them for hours, fixing each in turn in her mind. She wanted to know them, waking or sleeping. The shape of each face, the stance of each body, the individual habits of movement: all of these were written in the depths of her soul.

From time to time their gaze strayed over towards her, so she could feel herself part of the group. She felt included in their society. She no longer shrank away from the possibility of contact.

But try as she might to convince herself, she could never be entirely sure that they knew she was there. At best, perhaps, they might feel her as a passing shadow briefly interrupting the sunlight.

Finally, as the sun set, and the infant dozed off in the curvy adult's arms, full of nourishment, she let herself drift away. In her fantasy, she was being cradled alongside it.

She had eaten, and she slept, and she changed.

The Mirror sent off the remaining batch of observations that the lady had made, the ones that had never been committed. After that it compiled a summary report on the level of detail she was now able to achieve, and the extent to which she could engage emotionally with the world outside. It was all broadly in line with expectations. In any case, it needed to bring about a great deal of change in her while she slept.

The world outside, with its fleeting years, took no notice of her sleep, and changed even more rapidly than she did.

Richard Abbott

Instar 3

.

THE LADY WOKE, feeling sleek and well rested. She was hungry, but not with the urgency she had felt before. She lay peaceably on her bed for a time, assessing within herself what had changed. Her digits were more accurate and nimble than before, and as she flexed them she knew herself better able to carry out delicate work.

Her thinking was sharper as well. She thought back to all that she had experienced before falling asleep. The memory of the family round the fire was crystal clear, gathered together outside their wooden house towards nightfall. Their faces were still vivid to her internal sight, each unique and special to her. Enhancing the memories of the family members themselves was a layer of newly-provided knowledge about social dynamics.

The largest one was a male, she concluded, after considering his actions and attitudes towards the others. The other adult was female, probably his mate. They were almost certainly the mother and father of the smaller ones. The new web of information had many gaps, and presented the family purely in terms of mutually dependent relationships. She knew there had to be more, but this was good enough for now.

She resolved to use her new mental acuity to negotiate with the Mirror. She would persuade it to let her go out and meet these people. She would visit their house, learn to speak their language, and join their way of life. She would help them make better tools. She would take them a gift: not just the single flower she had thought before she slept, but a whole bunch. In return, she would ask the woman to become her mother as well. It would be a fair trade.

There was no time to waste. She had spent quite enough time sleeping since she saw them last. She knew their habits, and was quite sure that by now the father would be at work outside the house. She grabbed a carton of sap concentrate and wriggled as quickly as she could into the main room.

The couch had been reshaped again. Instead of the two sticks which had been there before she slept, there was a console with little grooves and bumps. She would have to learn how to use it. When she lay down now, her first two sets of limbs would be free to work with the new device. Once again, the game had changed.

As she settled herself in the couch, dim shapes on the pearly silver surface of the Mirror shimmered into a proper view. She stared at it. It looked all wrong. Nothing was familiar. She shook her head. The Mirror was simply viewing a different scene.

"This is the wrong place, Mirror. Show me where I was last night. Show me my family again."

There was no answer, except for a complete assurance that the location was the same. She found herself trembling, and the little crochet hook claws on her secondary limbs gripped the couch more tightly. She ran quivering fingers around the console, finding out how to move the view this way and that.

As she studied the outlook, a creeping sense of horror oozed through her body. The Mirror was right. The ridge of hills along the horizon was the same. So was the winding river in the valley down from her towers. Just there rose the hillock where she had first seen smoke. But the fireplace was quite gone, and the wooden house. The trees had been felled in a wide strip, pushing the forest well back from the riverbank. In its place was a wide green sward, and a rough track ambled through it, clinging to the base of the knoll.

Further back, in place of the widely scattered woodland huts she knew, a hundred houses huddled together. Smoke plumes rose from a hundred roofs and drifted away downstream. A set of raised banks crowned the ridge above them, white chalk showing like scars through the turf.

Anxiety filled her voice.

"Where has my family gone, Mirror? Why can't I see them?"

In the silence, terrible facts invaded her. Two thousand years had passed while she slept. Eighty generations of fleeting lives had come and gone. Her family, even the infant, had long since been scattered into dust and air. She was all at once confronted with death, with irrevocable loss. She curled up in a tight ball and howled, desolate.

The cold flow of information continued, and she could not block it out. The land had known change and migration, feast and famine, and the catalogue of years leaned heavily on it. The people outside carried only a tenuous connection with those she had known. Their heritage had been diluted, and little of them was left. The thread that joined them was exceedingly thin.

She uncurled a little when she heard that, senses thrilling at the faint hope. The link, then, was thin, but not broken. The connection was tenuous, but not absent. She stretched out again and poised herself over the console.

"Show me how to use this, Mirror, and I will search everywhere until I find them."

There was a clear sense of negativity and the permanence of death. This was followed by a barrage of data about heredity, and the rate of decline of any single inherited characteristic. She ignored the tirade, clinging to the remote possibility of reunion.

"But you will show me how to work this. I know you need me to use it. This is my private search, which I shall do alongside the tasks you set me."

After a brief pause, systematic knowledge of the device filled her. As before, it was only a start, and she would need to learn other skills for herself. She smiled thinly: it was a minor victory, but she had insisted on her own will, and won.

She spent the rest of the day learning the console's new features. For the first time she could look back at her house, reflect on what the outside world would see of her.

"Grey walls and grey towers is all they see of my life: never the garden and its flowers. How surprised they will be when I show them."

The courtyard, which seemed open to the sky when she visited it herself, was covered by a veil. The Mirror would not, or could not, let her see past it from outside. She supposed that it would be the same for others, if they chose to walk along the ridge and look down at her.

The whole building was on an eyot, dividing the stream. Dappled water passed by on either side, throwing the sunshine back in little flashes as it flowed. To her delight, the grassy banks between the water and the walls were full of flowers. They were the common plants of this world, not the exotic ones of her own, but nevertheless it was a gift. Perhaps the delights she enjoyed were starting to spill out from the narrow space she dwelt in.

It was late spring outside, so the Mirror told her, and the air was warm. She guided the Mirror's view through the woodland glades and saw the purple flowers pushing through last year's leaf litter. Small insects busied themselves around them, and she took the view right in to gaze at the intricacy of their bodies. Each proboscis plunged deep into the bell of petals, and a dust of pollen clothed them as they moved on. She considered her own mouth, her own limbs, and wondered about her origins.

As her vision roamed freely among the trees, her hands were busy on the console. The movements to tag what she saw, and to dispatch the observation once complete, needed very little thought, and her fingers rattled against the ridges and grooves, to and fro, to and fro. The Mirror no longer rewarded her with little plays of sound and light, but instead kept a running total of what she had done in the top corner. Time stretched out. She played games with it, trying to achieve a new high score, or to produce increasingly long chains of linked tags.

But always, after each passage through the trees, she would go back to the village. She discovered by accident that the Mirror's view was not blocked by the walls of houses. Perhaps it had always been so; she had never thought to try. But once she was aware of this, she went systematically through every room of every house, cataloguing all that she saw. They had metal now, where her family from before had only had wood and stone.

The Mirror still did not pass on to her the sounds of the things she saw. It ignored her pleas, leaving her uncertain whether what she asked was even possible. So, as before, she made up her own names. But when she saw the whole group gathered one night in a circle, lips and mouths moving in unison, she asked the Mirror what was happening.

Apparently they were singing, and she was suddenly given knowledge of what that meant. She knew, all in a moment, the movements of body and breath that made it possible. She studied the rapt faces the other side of the Mirror. In this moment, they were transcending their separateness and becoming a single organism.

Her mind was made up: she would sing too, and use the songs to unite with the village.

From that point on, she sang each day, whether the people were in view or not. It made her self-conscious at first, and she felt riddled with doubt about the quality of her voice. But then she reasoned that since neither could hear the other, it could hardly matter. The main thing was to join herself in spirit with them. One day in the future, when she finally met them, and learned how they spoke, she would concern herself with matching their tone.

Meanwhile, it was something else to occupy her fantasies. Was that mother singing as she sat beside her infant, working with a needle to patch some clothes? Were those men singing to their herd beasts as they worked side by side across a field, scratching at the surface to plant seeds? She did not know, and so she sang to please her own moods, and imagined that her songs fitted whatever she was seeing in the Mirror.

But all unknown to her, her voice slipped out from behind her walls, and spilled like a faint echo of the river's song across the eyot and over to the farther shore. Passers-by listened to the leaping sounds, and whispered to each other of places where another world came close.

"It is a goddess of the running waters," said some. "A queen in exile," said others, and a few just sighed, aching in their heart for the loss of a place they had never known.

She did not hear that, but she saw how people came out from the village to look at her walls, or kneel with arms out-stretched and faces turned up to the sky. A cairn of pebbles started to grow where the bank came closest, and when it was waist-high they left gifts there, little offerings out of their meagre possessions. At night, the birds and the shy forest creatures took some of the things and left others.

At the time when the daylight was longest they held some sort of festival beside the cairn, feasting and dancing while the sun's rays lit up the valley in a golden glow. The sound of their celebration echoed around her walls and, more faintly, into her courtyard.

"They do this for me, Mirror. They like me to be here."

She lifted up her voice and sang with them, and for the first time realised that they could hear her. A wave of surprise and awe washed over all the faces, front to back.

"But why can I not hear what they say, Mirror, when I look through you into their homes? Make it so I can hear them. And I want to go outside and meet them. Really outside, I mean. You must let me go out there."

But again, all that came to her was the sense of doom. The change would be unbearable. It must not happen.

She ignored the Mirror then, and sang along with the people until the sky was dark, and they lay sleeping in groups on the dewy grass. She watched them in the starlight, her view of them still clear in the gloaming because of whatever sense the Mirror used. She moved here and there as though walking among them, and dreamed of a day when she could do that in truth.

She studied every face in the hope of seeing the features of the family from before – her family – but could not persuade herself that any of the sleepers had more than a passing likeness to them.

Part way through the night, the moon rose, its first quarter bright over the land. She looked out across the open sward, thinking to stray briefly away from the crowd, and wander instead among the night creatures. There was always something new to tag for the Mirror, there amongst the shadows of the trees.

But as she started to move off, her hands already nimble on the console, a movement caught her eye. Two of the young adults nudged each other, got up, and moved slowly, covertly, towards the stream. Curious, she abandoned the woods and followed them.

They came to the shallow part of the river, where in daylight the sun threw back bright shards of light from the rippled water. It was a man and woman, she saw, supporting each other in the places where the stones were slippery. The man's beard was still youthful, and the woman moved with none of the stiffness which affected the older people she saw. She recognised the couple; they had been the focus of a ceremony in the centre of the village a few days before.

They reached the shore of the eyot. It was her own shore, she abruptly realised, switching her perspective back from that of the sleeping villagers. The couple pushed through the flowering grass, close up against the grey towered walls. They undressed each other – unnecessary, she thought, since the water had scarcely gone over their knees – and lay down facing each other.

She moved her point of view beside them, as though kneeling at their side. It was a difficult task, with them being so close to the impenetrable face of stone, but she persevered with delicate fingers. Then she watched them without comprehension while they were both tender and urgent with each other. After a time they lay still again, content, laughing together at things she could not see. Then finally they got up again, dressed, and went hand in hand to the far side, uncaring this time about the water's splash.

She got up from her couch and turned away from the Mirror. Its surface faded to shadowy silver as she squirmed away from it, away and out into her own garden. She went up and down the paths, stirred up in spirit but bewildered at her lack of comprehension about the couple's behaviour. To quieten her quick pulse, she took deep breaths of the fragrance around her, revelling in the night-scents lifting from the blooms. Finally, she thought to question the Mirror.

It filled her with information about reproductive processes, until she felt bombarded with biology. The anatomy she had seen made sense now, but she was still at a loss to understand the unrestrained delight. She gave up in the end, pulling herself away from the unsettling mystery. She lay beside her favourite blossoms and looked up at the heavens. To the south-east, a new luminary with a long tail hung. It had been brightening for several weeks, rising higher above the horizon every night. She murmured to herself, or else to the sky.

"It is a bearded star: perhaps it is a young star."

The Mirror, presumably imagining that she wanted to know about it, began to pour astronomical details into her. But she turned her head away and hushed it again. She wanted to hear no more tonight. In that moment, she longed to immerse herself in the night just as the young lovers had done. But she was alone, and there was nobody who could be beside her.

The days and the weeks went by. Every day she roamed a little further from her walls, gathering information for the Mirror with quick movements of her hands. She passed unnoticed through the woodland glades, and balanced unseen on the steep chalky banks of the hilltop gathering place above the village. She went in and out of houses, clicking and tapping the console as she recorded everything she saw.

Every so often, she was convinced that the people knew she was there. Sometimes as she lay watching them in their houses in the evenings, or as they rested in the heat of the day and ate some simple meal, she would notice one or other of them look about uneasily, or glance directly to where the Mirror's viewport was positioned. It happened more predictably if she gazed too long at any one of them.

They held occasional ceremonies on the river bank opposite her walls, always matching some key event in the lunar cycle. But one evening the young couple came by themselves. It was nearly three months after they had crossed over to her eyot. They stood on the further shore, waved and called out. The man placed some small trinkets on the cairn, and they bowed down in solemn manner.

It made no sense to her, but she accepted it as part of their ways. Then the woman unlaced her tunic and placed one hand on her belly, standing half naked and proud beside the flowing stream. She watched them, curious, until after a while they turned and went back towards the village. She lay on her couch for a long time after they had gone, aware that she had witnessed something significant, but feeling entirely ignorant.

They came back each week after that, as the twilight fell, at each of the moonphases. Week by week as she watched them, she realised that the woman's abdomen was changing. It was more rounded, and her skin tone had changed as well. And then all at once, the clues she was seeing fitted with the biological knowledge supplied by the Mirror, and she knew that the woman was pregnant. Their repeated visits abruptly made sense.

"Mirror, they think that somehow I helped them to get with child. They want to thank me for this."

There was no reply. She had not expected one, but she felt herself to be in an unknown world and wanted guidance.

"They bring me gifts. Mirror, are they right to think this? Might I have helped them in some way? Just by being here?"

She rolled restlessly from side to side, tapping pairs of feet together to help her think.

"I want to meet them, Mirror. The family I knew long ago, before I slept, were like a mother and father; these young lovers are like my brother and sister. I must go out and meet them, and we can be joyful together."

But although the reply held no words, there was the same sense of implacable refusal, like a hedge of thorns all around her chamber. She huffed, irritably, and scurried out into her garden to bury herself in her flowers.

Months slipped by, through the haze of summer into the fruitfulness of autumn. Her brother and sister came every week, without fail all through that time. The woman grew larger in girth each time, and her walking became slower. Then one day they were not there. She waited all evening, unable to move her focus away from the place by the cairn where they always stood. Nobody came.

The sun set, the quarter moon rose a little later, and she could not bear to drag herself away. She stayed watching all through the night, as the distant stars wheeled overhead around their axis, until the dawn rose with the dew.

She was ravenously hungry, and gobbled some leaves as a snack before rushing back to her viewpoint. The forest creatures stirred in the distance, but she refused to be drawn away. She lay watching for a long time, until it suddenly occurred to her that if they could not come to her, she could go to their house.

Fumbling with the controls in a way that she had not done since first waking, she hastened along the river path to the village gate, and through to the house where the couple lived with the man's older relatives. She passed through the wall without stirring so much as a twig, and looked through each of the rooms in turn.

And there, in a shadowed recess at the back, lay the young woman, a tiny infant held close against her.

She pressed close in alongside mother and child, huddled there with the young man and other family members, watching the little one as it tried to find its mother's breast to suckle. She sighed, content with the scene.

Then the woman lifted her preoccupied gaze from the baby and stared directly at the lady. It was an extraordinary moment, as she felt herself recognised and welcomed into the house. She had no idea how these creatures could know she was there, but it was the best that could happen to her.

The woman said something to the young man, made a little gesture with her hands, and he looked around, puzzled. The woman nodded again, then turned the baby slightly to face the lady.

There was a long moment when the baby's unfocused stare crossed her own, and then she pulled herself away from the room, away from the house, away from the village, and flung herself back into her chamber. Her fingers were trembling on the console, and her breathing was ragged.

"I cannot bear this, Mirror. You have to let me go to them."

And without waiting for a reply – which she knew would never come – she hauled herself away from her couch and spent the rest of the day among her flowers.

For some time after that she spent blocks of time arguing with the silent, unmoved face of the Mirror. Sometimes she tried reason, constructing chains of logic which she thought unassailable. Sometimes she begged and pleaded. Sometimes she railed at it in fury. She stopped singing, in case self-denial might be effective. Nothing worked. All of her attempts achieved nothing.

Then she tried abject cooperation, tagging and classifying everything within a huge area centred on the village. She peered into the lairs of wolves and boars, and followed the skipping fauns as, ears twitching, they learned to run with the herd before winter came. She listed the last of the fading flowers and the first fruits of every bush.

Then, fingers aching at the end of the day, she returned to the village to watch her brother and sister, and the infant they had made. In the privacy of her heart, she was sure she had, in some unfathomable way, helped in its creation.

Exactly a month after she had first seen the baby, they brought it out to the cairn opposite and held it up to her in the evening. The woman placed an offering on the cairn, and the man threw something metal into the flowing stream. The little one did nothing, unable even to hold up its head, but her heart melted at the scene.

She sang again, breaking her self-imposed fast, and saw their faces light up with awe as they heard her.

Just a few nights later she found herself ravenously hungry, and gorged herself on the food all around. Only at the end of her feasting, when she lay exhausted in her chamber and looked around, did she realise what was happening. Soon she would sleep, and while she slept her body would go through another change.

She gasped with anguish. How many racing years would slip away between sleep and waking?

"But if I sleep, I shall never know what happens to my sister, nor my brother, nor the child I helped them make. I cannot bear this, Mirror. It is cruelty. You must let me be awake for longer. I want to see what happens to them."

There was no answer, but unquenchable hunger seized her again. She tried not to eat, but the desire was stronger than gravity, irresistible as wind, and she could not deny it. Great helpless tears rolled down her face even as she tore at great strips of leaf and swallowed brimming bowls of sap.

Heavy, and feeling full to bursting, she wallowed on her couch, desperate for nightfall to come. Would she be given even one more day, before the unstoppable urge to sleep overwhelmed her?

They came that evening, and held up the infant so she could see it. She sang again for them, and her song was full of both the beauty and the sorrow of the passing world. She watched the glow of wonder on their faces as they heard her. She knew what they could not, that this would be the last time she would see them, and she sang to bless them as the shortening day eased into night.

Long after they had gone, she lay looking at the riverbank where they had stood. The world was made up of shadows now. When her brother and sister next came, when they held up the infant for her to see, she would no longer be there. She would be lost in her own world of slumber and transformation, and the quick years of the world would roll unseen around her.

How long would they continue to come, she wondered, once the sound of her singing was gone? Would they think that she was lost to them, lost somewhere in the gloaming? She watched herself stuffing food into her body, slithering awkwardly, heavily, into her chamber, and she felt that her heart was breaking.

Instar 4

THE LADY WOKE AGAIN. She lay still in her sleeping chamber, wondering how much time had passed. It felt like a single night, but she no longer trusted her perception of time. She took stock of herself.

There had been minor changes to her physiology. Her fingers were a little more dextrous again. Her hindmost pair of stabilising limbs had withdrawn inside her body, and she wondered if it would feel awkward when she began to move about.

But the main change was, once again, in her psyche. She remembered everything from before, and was disappointed at some of her reactions. She had allowed the silence of the Mirror to unnerve her, and had failed to provide a good enough argument to secure her release. This time it would be different. For one thing, she would be careful not to reveal all that she intended. In retrospect, she was sure that the Mirror actively worked to frustrate some of her wishes. From now on, she would take from it what she needed, and would not trust it naïvely as she used to.

She moved, carefully at first but with increasing confidence, across to the Mirror and the couch in front of it. She stopped and examined the console. It was more complex again, with a sturdy rod which ran from side to side, mounted on little pivots. The main surface was smooth, without the ridges which had guided her fingers before. It would not be a problem: she knew she now had the mental and physical ability to manage it.

She twisted the length of her body onto the couch.

"Well, Mirror. It's time to look outside and see what has changed this time."

She closed her eyes as the Mirror supplied its usual abbreviated instructions. She was aware this time that it was not just giving information, but providing her fingers with the bodily memories they needed to use the console. Her shorter front arms would be tapping and stroking the panel with delicate movements, while the next pair back would be working the cross-rod to and fro. Impressed, she wriggled all her digits together; all at once, it seemed as though she had been using the device her whole life.

She looked around, curious about the space she lived in. She knew now that the Mirror looked after the interior with the help of little machines, which trundled here and there according to its whim. They pruned and trimmed, fertilised and weeded.

But that was of only passing interest to her. It was the outside which mattered. She stretched herself on the couch, feeling how it had been modified to accommodate her new body shape with two fewer limbs. Then she slid eager fingers along the panel, and the clouded silver in front of her dissolved into the view beyond the four towers.

She scanned quickly around the horizon to be sure she was still in the same place. The ridge was familiar, though it had worn down a little since she last looked. At one place the land had slipped away, leaving a scar which already looked old, its original rough edges softened by time and vegetation. The river still curled around her island, though it was deeper now than it had been. If the couple she called brother and sister were crossing it now, the water would be above waist-level.

The island was rampant with the growth of high summer, and it looked as though nobody had walked its shores for a long time.

On the bank, where the villagers had once raised a cairn for her, there was now a little circle of carved wooden pillars, with a roof made of interlaced rushes. Under its shelter, the rough heap of stones had been rearranged to form a rectangular plinth. They had capped it with a single stone block, left in its natural unsmoothed state. It was very large, and the people must have exerted considerable effort to assemble the whole structure. A pair of metal beakers stood on top of the flat stone. Inside the wooden ring the grass was smooth and flattened, but outside they had let it grow up, untrimmed and untended.

She poised her hands on the console. It was time to check what had happened to the settlement. She began the to-and-fro limb movement that the Mirror had taught her. There were long sweeps of the rod for major moves, delicate touches on the panel for closer work. She ambled along the river bank at much the same pace as one of the native creatures would walk, tagging things she saw with quick flicks of her digits as she went. It was only just after dawn, and the low sun was struggling to pierce through ragged clouds.

The path was well used, with wheel ruts making deep parallel scores. They held muddy puddles now, and the nearby plants glistened with water droplets. A little box flashed up near the top of the Mirror, then faded after telling her that rain had been falling most of the night. She supposed that the mud would be an impediment to travellers, but her viewport drifted above the surface without difficulty.

The fields began soon after her eyot, just past the river bend. The gap seemed deliberate, as though they wanted to leave the area around her home in something close to its natural state. That pleased her. She could see that there was a mixture of ripening grain and vegetables, with fruit trees and bushes scattered at irregular intervals. The fields were long and thin. Some were just a few paces from side to side, while others stretched further. Rows of large stones marked the borders.

She followed the track as it wound lazily around the shape of the land. A bird flew nearby and landed on one of the stones. It was small, rich brown in colour, with a pert upright tail and bright eye. She remembered tagging some of its remote ancestors last time around, as they had flitted through the woodland. She stopped to watch it, and as the clouds shifted to let the dawn light shine on it, it sang, a long trilling call. She gasped. It was the first sound that she had heard from this world.

"Little bird, make the song again for me."

The bird ignored her, gave no sign that it was the least bit aware of her. She watched, entranced, as it sang again, and then flew away among the shifting shadows. Now that she focused, she began to hear other noises as the day awoke.

"Mirror, is it true that I can now hear the sounds of the world outside?"

Somewhere inside her the knowledge arose that this was now true: while she had slept, the Mirror had refashioned some of its own internal workings. But she knew also that nobody could hear her, not this far from her walls and her couch. She was not really out here among the birds and the animals, the sky and the people. Here, she was less than a shadow. She was a voiceless spirit that could move at will but touch nothing: hear everything but remain dumb. She buried the thought deep within her, along with the determination that one day she would break free of all this.

Ahead of her, the track curled around a stand of scrubby bushes which she did not remember. And above them rose swirls of smoke; more smoke than she had expected from the population she knew. She was also becoming aware of a dis-organised babble of voices, of shouting and crying that made no sense to her. There was an unsettling urgency to the cries, and she stopped, fearful. Then common sense overtook her again. She was invisible and immaterial to the senses of these people, and when she had last seen them, they had possessed nothing which could harm her. She pressed on.

The houses themselves had been set alight. Some were ashes and ruin, others had escaped with lesser damage. Everywhere was smouldering. Men, women and children lay here and there in the lanes and alleys, their blood pooling around their twisted shapes. It was all quite horrible. From the far side the survivors were creeping back in, stopping here and there to bewail the fallen.

She stopped at the first house which was still alight, keeping well back from the last lapping tongues of flame. Her rational self knew that they could not harm her, but the instinctual part kept pressing her away. Her real body was too delicate, too easily harmed to stay close. She looked at the milling village, watching as grief and despair filled faces. She knew nobody: they were all strangers to her. Their clothing had changed from last time, but it still looked rough, simple. The weapons that the men clutched, the tools scattered here and there had altered a little, but were recognisable. These were smaller changes than the wrench she had felt last time.

A woman came up to the house, leading a child. Her hair had once been gathered in long braids, but they were untidy and ragged, with loose locks spilling from the horn rings which held them. Her striped tunic was mired with mud and grass stains where she had lain in hiding, and the hem was ragged where thorns had tugged at it. The boy stood and stared blankly as she beat out the flames before they could lick further into the roof-thatch.

She pulled at the door, and it scraped stickily open. She looked in, and her face twisted in anguish. The lady slipped through the thin walls to find out for herself what was inside. A man lay facing the door, just in front of the central hearth, with household knife and farm implement beside him. He was slashed with many wounds, and blood had spattered the rushes covering the earthen floor.

The woman wailed as she crossed to the body, a wordless cry of such misery and abandonment that the lady felt the harrowing in her own soul. She had never known bereavement in the fleeting days of her life, but she understood what it was to be left alone. The woman flung herself down full-length on the floor, pulling loose her braids and letting her hair spill out around her body, clutching at the dead man's broken hands. Moved by some impulse stronger than thought, the lady knelt beside her and joined her as she poured out her sorrow.

Five times they cried out together, while the boy watched silently from the door. Then the woman sat up, called the lad to her, and closed the man's eyes to stop them staring blindly up at the ragged gaps in his walls and ceiling. She gathered ashes from the cold household hearth, smeared them on her face and that of the child, rubbed handfuls into their hair, and then sat back, arm circled around him like a palisade. The lady wished she could do the same, but her arms could not touch, nor her body comfort. The sounds of the village trickled through the open door, noises of loss or unexpected restoration, of collapse or repair.

They sat there for a long time, until finally the woman sighed heavily and rose again. She dragged the man's body from the room, through the door, stopping often to rest. When she had nearly done, two others came to help, and the corpse was soon lying outside. The boy sat watching vacantly as his mother bundled both the spoiled reeds and the broken household goods outside the house. Then she started to clean, scrubbing frantically at walls and surfaces.

The lady watched her, wanting to help but powerless. Then she remembered that in truth she was lying prone on her couch, in front of the Mirror, and started to tag what she saw, her quick flicks on the console matching the jerky moves of the woman.

Beside her, the boy started fidgeting, casting uneasy glances around the room. Suddenly he got up and ran to his mother, a stream of words pouring from his mouth. The Mirror, it seemed, could provide sound but not understanding.

The woman stopped, looked at the boy, put her arms around him again, and spoke. He leaned against her, turned slowly to face every corner of the room, then pointed directly at the lady, his finger trembling. She had forgotten that these people had the uncanny ability to know when they were being watched.

The woman took two deep breaths, said something in a voice which quavered, lifting hesitantly at the end. Then she dropped the rag she was holding and sank to her knees. She hid her eyes behind one hand and pulled the boy down beside her with the other. The lady watched them curiously, remembering similar behaviour from the villagers from the time before she slept. It meant something to these people, this gesture.

It meant something for her, too. Because of something like this, in a former age she had helped her sister and brother to make a child between them. This time, she knew she was more cunning. This time, she would find a way to turn the outcome into something satisfying for both the villagers and herself.

She felt connected to the woman, and already knew that she would revisit often. She imagined, though, that the Mirror harboured suspicions. To allay these, she busied herself all over the vicinity during the days, arms swinging side to side for the big movements, fingers tapping on the console for the details.

She was forced to admit that the work was interesting, as she tried to deduce the years of history from the scattered evidence deposited during her sleep. More land had been cleared for crops and herds at some stage, she decided, and then abandoned. The determined woodland was trying to reclaim its own. Some animals and birds were more common than last time, pulled in like comets to the human centre, but others had become scarce.

She soon realised that the village had been attacked by an unexpected enemy almost immediately before her own awakening. She did not have the necessary experience to make sense of what she saw, but the Mirror added what she lacked. Groups of these people living in nearby places would steal from each other, unconcerned whether theft turned to brutality and murder. She was at first appalled, and soon afterwards outraged that such a thing would happen to her village.

Every day, as the sun set and the light failed, she returned with the people to their huddled cluster of houses. On that first day, the survivors had burned the bodies of their own people, scattered the ash around the houses, and started to build little remembrance cairns here and there among the fields. They dragged the outsider corpses to the edge of the forest, stripped them naked, and left them there as carrion. Their weapons were gathered up, bent, broken or notched beyond use, and thrown into a reedy bend of the river.

Unexpectedly, she felt a fierce sense of approving justice rise up in her. If her hands had permitted her to touch, she would have been pulling the clothes from the corpses with all the others. Since she could not do that, she watched in vigil through the night, and was satisfied when bird and beast came and tore eyes and flesh apart.

By the end of the first week, the outside of the woman's house had been restored. The lady drifted around and through the circle of the walls, admiring the neat willow wattles and the external daub. Here and there, new thatch replaced parts which had been burned. The interior was neat, as though it had never been violated. Fresh reeds covered the floor. Utensils were arrayed in careful rows, except when in use to prepare a small meal. But both woman and son still had ashes on their face, and the woman's hair was still ragged and wild, unbound.

The lady passed silently around the house, reaching out to the things she could not handle. She understood the function of most items – utensils for cooking, cleaning, personal hygiene, entertainment – even if they were necessarily shaped differently from those she used herself. Some made no sense to her, and she decided she would simply need to watch for a few days longer. Then, making a slow circuit round the curved outer wall, past the curtained sleeping section, she came to a wooden frame, standing vertically against the wall.

She studied it. It was clearly important to the woman: it was the first thing she had set to rights after cleaning the house, even though she had had to struggle against its weight. As well as the outer frame, some other wooden struts were pivoted to the sides and across the middle.

A curtain of loose fabric strands filled the interior, stretched taut by little weights. A strip of finished cloth ran from side to side across the top, its bold background colour blazoned with bright patterns. Horizontal threads traced in and out of the vertical ones, packed tightly against each other.

The first night, having taken pains to restore it, she had left it untouched, and simply retired to her sleeping mat. On the second night, she had stared at it for a while, and then turned away. Both nights she had held the boy close until he dozed, and then lay awake herself for a long time, staring across the empty room. She pulled woollen cloths across her and pushed them away again, bundled up hay and flattened it, and eventually settled. But the lady saw that every passing sound, every night noise of animal, each louder gust of wind jerked her awake. She had not slept well.

This night, she settled the boy sharpening all of the household tools, and turned to stand by the frame. She stood there, holding the long strands of fibre in one hand, and a wooden paddle in the other, irresolute. The boy asked something, his childish voice curious. She made a little noise, non-committal, then finally took the paddle and started tapping the lower edge of the coloured band.

She worked away at it steadily, systematically, alternately working coloured thread from side to side, adjusting the position of the cross-beam, and firming the loose threads into a tight mass of woven cloth. As she worked, her face relaxed, her eyes looked further away than the cloth which was building in front of her, and her breathing slowed to a steady pulse. The patterns of sound grew steady, rhythmic. Her hands moved easily to and fro, to and fro, and all at once the lady realised that these were the same movements that she herself made for the Mirror.

She pulled herself out of the house, back to the four grey walls where she was real, letting herself feel the firmness of the couch she lay on. She looked at the console in front of her, moved her hands in the patterns she knew so well. Except for the fact that she was prone rather than standing, they were the same. The revelation teased at her.

"Mirror, I make patterns just like she does. But why? And for whom? For you? For somebody else?"

Knowledge bubbled up in her out of the Mirror's habitual silence. She had come to expect that it would not be enough, but it was something. The patterns she made went elsewhere: the Mirror was simply the vehicle through which they were channelled to others. She had an impression of immense distance, but no sense of direction or place.

For the time being she accepted the partial answer, and kept secret from the Mirror her determination to know more. She flitted back along the track to the woman's house, back through the wall. In the short time that she had been away, the boy had fallen asleep, utensils scattered beside him. The sharpening stone had fallen from his hand.

The woman was still at her work, eyes dreamy and far away. The lady watched, breathless, seeing her arms following their well-learned pattern, recognising the quick flicks of the fingers.

And as she stood there, feeling kinship quicken in her soul, the woman's eyes came back into focus, and she was looking directly at the lady. Her hands trembled, her lips quivered slightly, but this time she carried on working. She said something, questioning, hesitant. Of course it meant nothing, and once again the Mirror's constraints frustrated her. She could neither understand the words, nor reply to them. She could only stand there, mute, hoping that comprehension might come in time. The woman started working at her cloth again, but every so often she would glance up, her eyes still full of uncertainty.

The days started to fit into their own larger pattern. For much of the day she scoured the countryside for new things to tag, sending them away in flurries to their unknown destination. She worked the console with the ease of habit, limbs and digits moving swiftly, smoothly. As the sun declined towards the horizon she returned to the same house. The boy was not usually there until the middle evening, and spent his days in a different place with another three lads and an older man. It looked as if he was being trained in the skills of metalwork. When he got back, he was exhausted, and fell asleep very soon after eating. Unlike the desperate nights immediately after the attack, the woman settled him back into his own bed, keeping him away from her own.

Then, after she had arranged him tidily to sleep, and put back the few things which were out of place, she would return to her fabric. The strip of made-up cloth grew slowly longer. The patterning suggested birds and flowers, but they were disguised in odd twists and curls that flowed around each other in lively shapes.

After the first few fearful days, the woman started talking as she worked, a thin stream of chatter which never seemed to expect an answer. The lady shivered with excitement when she first understood that she was included in the intercourse. It was like the conversations she heard the men carrying out in the fields, or the women around the well. She could listen, even if she could not reply.

Slowly she worked out what some of the words signified. She bounced back to her home after an evening of break-through, babbling away to the Mirror as she wriggled off the couch and unwrapped her meal of leaves and berries.

"She is a weaver. She works on a loom, Mirror, that's what she calls the thing that she uses to make her cloth. The frame. The wooden structure in her house that looks just like this console I lie at. A loom, she called it. So I work on a loom as well, Mirror. And the things I tag and that you send off are like the pattern she weaves. I wonder if it looks so bright, so nice as the one she makes. I would like it to be pretty. If only I could see what the finished cloth looks like. What do you think, Mirror? Shall I call myself a weaver now?"

Another night, a week or two later, she was slower, more reflective.

"I think that she is lonely, Mirror. Also, she is still afraid that those wicked enemies will come back and hurt the village again. And although a whole moon cycle has gone by, she still longs for the man who she lost. I think that her leaders have said that the time for giving sorrow to the dead is over. She has cleaned her clothes and hair now, and the boy's as well, but I am sure that inside she has not changed. I don't know how long she will stay like that. Can a person grieve for longer than a month? I have no idea."

She paused briefly while the Mirror started to inform her of mourning customs, but shook her head and all of her limbs together when the explanation started to become lengthy.

"Well, I know that she wants him back. But when she talks, sometimes it is as though she would have another person to replace him. It is when she wakes, anxious, in the night, and I see her breathing quicken with fear at an unexpected noise. I hear her whispering, Mirror, though I expect she thinks that nobody hears her. She asks for someone that will be with her, who will be loyal and true to her. Do you think she is asking me, Mirror?"

She paused, pondering.

"I have nobody like that. I have nobody loyal and true. But maybe she needs such a person more than I do."

But she craved companionship herself, and did not believe her own words.

Abruptly conscious that she was revealing much more of herself to the Mirror than she had intended to, she stretched out on the couch again and threw herself out into the darkness, tagging owls and bats as they occupied the wooded night. The thought of somebody, loyal and true, who would be beside her when the time came to leave the Mirror behind, had become very appealing. Perhaps she could work with the woman so that they could find such a companion together.

"Mirror, you have told me that I cannot leave this place in my own body. But can I bring this woman into my home? I want to show her my house. I see into hers: she should see mine. Else it is not fair."

The lady was moving in restless sinewy circles round her room, feet tapping and clacking on the floor, nibbling through a handful of assorted berries. She stopped in frustration at the clear tone of rejection which came back to her, then resumed her pacing. Little clusters of rapid taps rippled around her room as she circled the console.

"But why? You never tell me why."

Breathing would not work, she heard. The air that was life to her, was death to the villagers, and vice versa. The lady refused to believe it.

"I do not accept that I am so different to them. This world is all I have known, ever since I opened my eyes and took my first breath. It makes no sense, Mirror. You are keeping some part of the truth from me. If I am of this world, and they are too, how can it be that the air we each breathe is harmful to the other? And you yourself once said that one day I would not be so different to them. That was back when I first met my family."

She noticed the Mirror's stream of information falter and then, almost immediately, restart when she spoke of her beginnings. This, then, was the source of the deception. A little tingle of anxiety pattered inside her. She already knew that she was insubstantial to the villagers and that she could pass through substance at will. Outside of these walls neither person, nor bird, nor animal could properly see her. Perhaps in truth she was no more than a fiction, an incorporeal figment, no more than somebody else's projection. Her fretful feet rattled on the floor, until she seized on a memory of song, a memory of the last time around.

"My brother and sister heard me sing in the time before they made their child. The people heard me sing when they came to the riverbank. We sang together. Surely I am like them? Surely I am as real as they are? I am not just a shadow. I'm not."

She felt tentative acceptance from the Mirror, but knew that it was still holding something back. The truth she was given was always partial, always qualified. She flung herself full-length on the couch and, before hurling her intangible self beyond the looming walls, screamed at the unreceptive face in front of her.

"I'm half sick of shadows."

She pounded up and down the woodlands, following the animal tracks as they twisted among the trees. Her fingers drummed on the console, tagging the forest nightlife without conscious thought, hands moving to and fro like the woman at her loom. Her immaterial breath sighed, not stirring even the smallest leaves as she moved past them. Finally, ascending without effort the steep chalk banks, she stretched out on the ancient enclosure and looked down at the village.

She was angry at herself, she knew, more than at the Mirror. Once again, she had said more than she should, and had allowed the blank face of the Mirror to distort her emotions. How could continued silence draw so much out of her? This had to stop. The Mirror, she now knew, was no more than an intermediary. Somewhere else, somewhere far away, lived the ones who were really important. The Mirror was no more than a window to them. The patterns that she herself was building were for them.

From now on, she would remember that the Mirror was simply a tool, albeit a clever one. The Mirror had little machines that tended the plants and kept them thriving. They were mere adjuncts to the Mirror, with no life of their own: so also the Mirror must be simply a tool for somebody else. She must aim to please not the Mirror, but these mysterious others. If she did well by them, if she gave them what they seemed to want, perhaps they would reward her.

She gazed fondly for a while down at the woman's round house. The recent repairs to its thatch were clear in the light of the gibbous moon. Both mother and son had been sleeping when she left there earlier, before her confrontation with the Mirror. The boy had been restless, tearful, but after only a short time of comfort the woman had pushed him away and turned back to her own bed, hugging herself in her loneliness instead of him.

As she watched, the woman came to the door and looked out, this way and that. She took one step outside and stopped, holding on to her doorframe. She glanced across at one of the nearby houses, then briefly up to the ridge, but her gaze moved on again. The lady wondered, once more, if she was at all visible. Was there, perhaps, a glint of something shining on the slope? Or a place where the moonlight shimmered unexpectedly? Or perhaps, as sudden gloom shadowed her thoughts, there might be no outward sign at all. Down below, among the houses, the woman turned again in her hesitation, and went back inside.

The lady said not a word to the Mirror for over a week. She tagged everything she could find during the day, and again far into the night, making intricate connections between each item. It meant a lack of sleep, and a denial of regular eating times, but she decided that the cost was worth bearing. The remote beings who controlled both her and the Mirror would be impressed. It was another negotiation.

So, day by day, she was making patterns on her loom which grew steadily longer and more ornate, just like those on the woman's frame standing against the inside wall of her house. She had set aside the twilight to be her own time, as day yielded to night. She spent every evening in that home, listening to the woman as she chattered amiably. Day after day, the woman's ability to discern her presence was becoming more reliable.

The language was unfolding to her as she listened, though many of the words and phrases still meant nothing. Some things needed deep familiarity with village life, and for all her close observations, she knew she was still a stranger.

One night, when the woman seemed more preoccupied than usual and had less to say, she decided it was time for an experiment. Her usual habit was to wait until the woman had finished her work and settled in her solitary bed. She would squat beside her as she composed herself for sleep, then slip away like a dream. She was certain that the woman knew that she was there, and believed that her presence helped her to sleep more deeply than nature alone would allow. But she could do nothing about the tears that were shed in the darkness, and usually avoided them.

This evening, instead of remaining by the wall opposite the loom, she moved right up in front of it, and then moved deliberately towards the door. The woman blinked, distracted from her chatter. Her hands stilled on the loom. The lady moved towards her, then back to the door again. This time the woman took a step, two steps to follow, before halting again.

It took several attempts, but in the end the woman had opened her door and was standing on the threshold. She looked back at the sleeping boy, then closed the door quietly and followed the lady.

They went at walking pace along the rutted lane beside the river. The lady paused in every patch of moonlight to look back, imagining that this made her more real. The woman was sure-footed in the gloaming, and her initial hesitancy slowly yielded to a steady pace. Her eyes had the same placid, unfocused gaze as when she worked her loom.

The grey towers came into view on the river's eyot, and the woman nodded slightly. She understood where she was going, and pushed up beside the lady, eager now to finish the journey. She stopped briefly inside the wooden pillars, to touch the stone block with careful fingers. Then, with a long breath and clenched hands, she hitched up her skirt, stepped into the flowing chill of the stream, and waded across.

The lady went back into her body and used the Mirror simply as a window, not a wandering viewport. She was hesitant at first through lack of use, but then she started to sing. The woman flinched at the unaccustomed sound, then prostrated herself among the grass and flowers.

The lady wanted to use the words she had learned, but did not know how to fashion them into ideas. So she kept herself as wordless as birdsong, a pure melody which she hoped would communicate the longing in her soul. Her desire was for the woman to join her in the singing, not lie there as though crushed by it.

Her voice faltered a little. It was still pure as the nightingale's call, but the purity was tinged with frustration and sorrow. The woman raised her head at the change of tone, scanning the windowless walls. She sat up and smoothed her clothing, waited for a hollow space in the threads of sound, and then said something.

The lady, limbs quivering with excitement, replied in the language of the village. She wondered how she sounded to the other; perhaps like one of the reed pipes they played by the firelight in the evenings. The idea of being a musical instrument brought to life appealed to her, and a peal of happy laughter rippled through her words. The woman might not understand what she was saying, but the emotion resonated between them. For a while, the woman was her mirror.

She tried using the little she had learned – working at the loom, walking among flowers, living with somebody loyal and true – but it was not long before the words ran out. She was less fluent than she had thought. But the woman nodded, alive with recognition. She stood up then and slowly walked the circuit of the walls, one hand trailing lightly along the rough stone. There was no door, no arched entryway into the keep, and no windows on the flanks of the towers. At one place, she ran her fingers up and down a vertical crack in the sheer face of rock, but could find no key to open it. The keep was only small, and it did not take long for her to return to her starting point.

The lady sang again, retreating from the words which had promised so much but delivered so little. This time when she fell silent, the woman bowed her head and backed away from the walls. She waded across the stream, stumbling in some of the deeper places, and knelt inside the ring of wood. Then she called out three times before setting off towards the village. She looked back several times until the sweep of the road hid her. The lady eased back on the couch, letting her go, her whole body trembling with the thrill of what had happened.

"You see, Mirror, it is possible for me to befriend them. That woman knew I was in her house, and she came out to mine. Next time I want you to let her inside the walls, so that we can be together properly. She is my friend, and together we will both find somebody loyal and true."

As usual, the Mirror radiated rejection. They could never meet. They could never be together. What was life to one was death to the other.

"I think you are jealous, Mirror. You do not like it that I make friends outside of these walls. You make up reasons to try to stop me."

She flounced away from the console before another reply could come. She clattered round the interior of the building. She was not going to tell the Mirror, but she was intrigued by the fault that the woman had found in passing. It was on the side of the building that she did not normally visit, and she had overlooked it before.

She went out into the garden, letting her fingers trail happily through the fragrant petals, trying to orient her position against the outside world.

The place where the woman had crossed the river was to her left, she thought. That meant that the crack, or crevice, or whatever it was, was on the right. She pushed through blossoming shrubs, trying not to be distracted by the delightful feeling of pollen dusting her skin. She had never before gone all the way across here, but had always been drawn aside by the flowers and fruit which hung like charms in the heavy air. It was an intoxicating place, and she struggled to resist the sensory lure.

Behind the last of the bushes was the wall. Creepers clung to it, running far up the walls towards the shining roof. But lower down, reaching only just above her head, hung a curtain of loosely woven cloth. The busy tendrils gripped it here and there, and the folds stirred gently as the mechanical breeze pushed at them. She eased aside a place where two folds over-lapped. The stone wall stared back at her.

It was finished just as carefully as the rest of the building, and the reasons why it was so carefully concealed were not clear. She wriggled further into the gloom, trying to see if there was anything unusual. She could hear one of the Mirror's little machines at work nearby, busy tending the vegetation. She quietened her hasty feet, wanting it to move on without finding her. This was not like the journeys outside the keep, where her presence was less substantial than a shadow. Here, she was real, and could actually be found out.

She held her breath as the machine moved closer, then further away again. Perhaps she had not been discovered. She pushed on again, eager fingers moving over the smooth rock. She found nothing. The space was small in here, and cramped, and she found it difficult to get air. The confined space gnawed at her self-control, and the noise of the Mirror's machine started to creep closer again. Blood pounding inside her, she forced her way back out, away from the narrow space, back into the open and the flowers. She grabbed at a cluster of low-hanging fruit and gulped at the berries, swallowing them almost whole, trying to steady herself. Then she ducked back through the bushes and tried to stroll nonchalantly back down the path to her room.

She lay there in the cosy gloom for a long time, trying to retrieve a sense of strength and resolve. Next time she attempted that, she would have to be much better prepared.

A week later she tried again. In the waiting days, she kept herself enthusiastically busy with the Mirror's activity. One day she worked her way downstream along the river-bank as far as she could before the light faded. The trees unfolded eventually into a boggy expanse, where dry grassy knolls swelled upwards towards the cloudless sky. She found occasional settlements across the wetlands, but could not tell if these were the people who had violated the village she called home.

When the sun eased into the marshes, and the night creatures started to pipe their shrillness to the twilight, she turned her gaze upwards to the vault of stars. Somewhere amongst them was the place where her messages could rest. She could not imagine it as anything other than a copy of her own keep. She supposed that another Mirror received all that was sent, locked inside a square of walls and towers. Perhaps another her reclined on another couch, watching another list of tags go past. But to what end?

She snorted. It was a waste of time thinking about it. She must focus herself on the task of finding a way out of the enclosing walls, meeting the woman from the village, and arranging for them both to find companions who would be loyal and true. She released her grip on the console, and let the marshes, the stars, and the night noises dissolve. They were all just shadows.

She snatched a quick meal and then, with juice still staining her tongue and greedy fingers, went out again into the night. The woman was at her loom, looking at nothing, hands moving in their ingrained pattern. As the lady passed into the house she paused briefly in her work. A little smile brightened her face. She bobbed her head, then started talking in a hasty buzz of words. The loom clattered and clacked behind all that she said, and the lady struggled to understand even one word in ten. It was all too much, and she felt overburdened by the noise.

She escaped again into the quiet night, and found that the woman had followed her. Indeed, she was already starting along the river path, and as she got further from the village she became increasingly animated. The lady moved at her usual even, steady rate, but her companion skipped and bounced along the track as though imitating the children when they played in the open fields between chores. It was all quite incomprehensible.

They arrived at the keep together, and as before the lady sang. The woman listened attentively, but with an air of impatience. As soon as there was a gap she broke in, rapid sentences rushing across the space between them. It was all much too quick, much too unsettling, but the lady caught occasional words in the stream. She was almost sure that the woman was talking about a companion, one who would be loyal and true, and there was a question which she kept repeating, over and over again. Most of the words were lost, but there was enough that she was sure of.

"Oh," she trilled in excitement, "Oh, yes yes yes, we will find companions together, loyal and true, just as soon as I find my way out of this place. Yes."

The woman's face lit up with delight, and she prostrated herself in the flowering grass. Then leaping up again, she splashed across to the other shore and ran back towards the village.

It was strange, and abrupt, but the lady had her own preparations as well. She slithered out into the courtyard. The Mirror's spying machines were dormant just now, and the garden lay in shadows.

She felt her way over to the hidden stretch of wall by touch and starlight, ducking and pushing past the curtains of vines. There was no moon just now. With everything in gloom, she did not feel the oppression of the confined space so acutely, and could marshal herself to stay there. Her breathing was ragged, and every last fibre of her self was stretched taut, but she was able to set that aside and explore.

She squeezed into the narrow gap, working her way finger by finger until she came to the sharp corner. There was nothing. She had no room to turn, so began wriggling backwards.

One of her rear feet became wedged in a cluster of roots, and she felt panic bubble up in her throat and mouth. She felt dizzy. Her thoughts started to whirl, and her mouth opened to shriek. Only the thought of the listening Mirror stopped her.

She pressed a hand into her mouth and chewed on it fiercely, holding doggedly onto her self-control. Very slowly, she eased the foot forwards again, out of the root's clench. It was free. She sighed, feeling anxious trembles running up and down her whole body. Then, even more slowly, she lifted the foot higher, and twitched it back towards the open space again. A moment's struggle, and it was past the blockage. She took a step, and another step, and before long she was back to her starting point.

Every part of her wanted to run away, back to the security of her room and its comforts. But she refused herself that, turned, and pressed on in the other direction. Her foremost limbs caressed the wall, reaching up and down as far as she could reach. Step by step she went along the wall, until suddenly she found something. There was an edge, a discontinuity running up and down. She tried to place herself in relation to the outside world, but the effort defeated her. The notch might correspond to the one that the woman had found outside, or it might not.

She moved further, and found a circular pattern. It was too dark to see, so she ran eager fingers around it, testing the shape of it. It was a dial, she was sure, with a sort of hand grip in the middle. There were shapes picked out in relief beside the grip. Perhaps it held the secret of opening the wall: she could not tell. She would need to revisit it in daylight, when the patterns might yield their meaning.

She eased backwards, slowly and cautiously. She hated the cramped space, and her anxious breathing was loud and tattered. It would not do to get trapped here. The Mirror would be able to rescue her once the sun came up, with the help of its little army of drones, but that would surely give away her secret. And she was not sure she could survive until morning; a madness of panic would consume her long before that.

There was a fearful moment as she squeezed past a place where the folds of the curtain had bunched up against a shrub, and then she was out. She wanted to rush straight to her couch, flit through to the village, and impart the happy news to the woman, but she needed to ground herself first. Together they could start their joint quest for companions, but before that she would look to herself.

She ate and drank, savouring the wealth of tastes. Perhaps this would be her last meal alone, and she wanted everything about it to be memorable. She quaffed an entire carton of the nectar she loved best, and gorged herself on ripe fruit. It was splendid.

Finally, replete, and with the difficult spaces beside the wall pushed away from her thoughts, she moved across to the Mirror. It radiated negativity. Both entering and leaving the keep would mean doom.

Apparently it had detected her investigation of the wall, and she struggled for equanimity. Was there nothing beyond the Mirror's inquisitorial sight? She would not apologise to it, nor accept that she had done anything improper. There was nothing to be ashamed of. Surely there was not.

"I am going to visit the village, Mirror."

Without waiting for an answer, she stretched out on the couch, gripped the controls and flung her vision out into the night. She moved faster than her friend might run, faster than the shadow of the owl flitting beneath the rising moon.

The woman was not in her house. The boy was sleeping, but the woman's bed was empty. The lady was sure that she had not passed her along the track. She went back outside and circled the building.

Then she heard the woman's voice, coming from inside another house. It was the one she had looked at uncertainly, that night when the lady watched from the chalk ramparts up on the hill.

She went over to it, puzzled, and passed through the walls. The woman was in there, seated at a table opposite the man who lived there. She was squeezing his hands. Their faces were very close. She was talking, in a low, husky voice quite unlike the one she had used outside the keep earlier.

The lady pressed close to hear her words.

"And the Lady in the tower gave her blessing when I went to her."

The man replied. His voice was deeper, more strongly accented, and she could not follow what he said. It was obviously a question.

"In the tower, on the eyot across from the holy place. But in her spirit she comes often to the village. I know when she comes into my house. And yes, she spoke to me when I called out for her counsel."

Another question. The woman paused before answering.

"In truth, I do not know if she is the goddess of the waters, or one of the Fair Folk. Or perhaps she is mortal like us, but pure and devoted to a vow of service. Maybe an ancestor from the deep past. But whoever she is, I believe that she means good for us, and I trust her word. She is no trickster, and bears no malice, I am sure."

Another question. His hands were gentle, and he caressed her face. She took a long breath.

"I asked her, and although I could not understand most of what she said, I heard her say 'yes yes yes'. Those words were most clear, as clear as the words that you say to me now. Three times, my heart, three times is the charm, and three times she said yes."

She stood up, but not to leave the house. Instead, she stepped around the table and stood by him, full of longing. He nodded slowly, then his face lit up with fulfilment.

The lady stood aghast as they moved towards the bed. There was a rustling of clothes, a mutual accommodation.

The lady could not bear to stay. She let slip her hands on the console and rolled this way and that on the couch. She howled in the empty room at the anguish of betrayal.

The woman must surely have understood that the quest was to be shared. To slip away and consummate her own choice, before the lady had even found out how to escape her walls, was a cruelty beyond comprehension.

She scuttled away from the couch, wracked by misery, and tottered round the uncaring room. Her ache could not be soothed; her heart could not be mended.

Finally, she turned to the Mirror, her face wet with the tears that streamed without stopping.

"I want to sleep now, Mirror. Give me what I need to leave this age behind. I will stay here no longer."

There was a pause.

It could be done, but outside the proper cycle there were risks. There could be unexpected costs.

"I don't care, Mirror. I want no more of this faithless time. I want to sleep, and while I sleep it will fade into the shadows."

After a long silence, there came a grudging acceptance.

A mechanical servant brought bits and pieces from somewhere. She watched it dully, half-aware that there must be store cupboards that she knew nothing of. There was the usual array of fruit and leaves, syrup and nectar. Alongside them was a carton of powder she had never seen before.

She mixed powder and nectar, then devoured the lot, uncaring of the bitter edge that the powder gave.

She ate, and she slept, and she changed.

Instar 5

THE LADY WOKE. She stretched, and wriggled, and started to assess what was different this time. Hardly anything on a physical level, she thought, but on the other hand her whole body was tingling with anticipation. She felt as though she was on the verge of some tumultuous change. Some unexpected twist in her life's path lay ahead, and she had no idea if it would be pleasant or unpleasant for her.

Her thinking was sharper once more, but was also filled with the knowledge of limitation. There was a kind of deep despair in her mind, a feeling of ultimate futility, constantly at odds with a surging sense of daring. She felt conflicted, torn in two by the paradox: boldness and anxiety confronted one another inside her. It would be, she suspected, a constant feature of this cycle of existence.

She now knew exactly which branch of stars her messages fled to, out in the golden galaxy. But the knowledge only brought her frustration now. Last time around she would have been elated, imagining that the information would give her power. But now she knew that it was just a destination address, and one so far away that the distance meant nothing. It was just a fact, stripped of any importance to daily life.

She considered the actions of her younger self. She had been foolish, clearly, in placing her trust in the villager before being able to communicate properly. That woman had seen her not as a fellow traveller through the world, but simply as a guarantor of promises. The notion of a shared action to find joint companions, loyal and true, had never occurred to her.

No matter: she had left that woman, her son, her chosen partner, and a whole way of life somewhere in the remote past. It was time to see what life was now like outside her walls.

She moved out from her sleeping chamber to the console. It looked very much as it had done last time. The fancy of still working at a loom pleased her. It connected her to a part of the last cycle that she remembered with delight.

"Mirror, what new things should I know?"

A little flood of information washed over her. It was partly verbal now: the Mirror was no longer just informing her at a subliminal level. It was more like speech; it was easier to follow sentences and threads of ideas.

"The early conclusion of the last cycle has delayed my plan for improvements."

She shrugged at the scarcely-veiled implication that it was her fault, and concentrated on the information being imparted. The console's physical form was unchanged, and the other ways in which it gathered information from the world around were different in only minor ways. She would still not be able to understand anything that the people were saying.

She did not comment on that, but inwardly she was disappointed. If only she could have spoken with the woman the last time around, perhaps the outcome would have been happier. But she kept her thoughts unspoken, not allowing her determination to go on exploring the dial in the wall to come too close to the surface.

She did not ask how long she had been asleep, but simply stretched herself out on the couch. The Mirror's surface clouded, then cleared again, and there was her valley.

Time had evidently passed. Where the pillared pavilion had stood, there was now a grey stone building, tidy, with a series of low mounds and upright markers clustered around it. She smiled: they had given it a squat square tower not unlike those of her own home. The grass on her eyot was now neatly trimmed, and there were neat rectangular flowerbeds.

The river was shallower again, and partly clogged with long reeds except where the current was swifter. A little boat was moored on the opposite shore. She presumed it was used by the gardener, and wondered if she would get the opportunity to meet him or her. The boat had no oars or sail, and was tethered with a rope which ran around a tree on either bank.

She supposed that the gardener simply pulled his ride across the flowing stream.

The line of trees had been pushed back again, and the ripening fields had swallowed the space. Out here the crops were of various grains: the ears were swollen and heavy, and most had already been harvested. The woods themselves were fading into brown leaf litter and bare branches. The bright green that she had known from earlier times had long gone, and the leaves had fallen which, she guessed, had been alight with yellows and reds. It was late autumn, and close to winter, and she had not woken at this season before.

Further away, the long chalk banks on the ridge had sagged, and their former whiteness was thickly clothed with greenery. They had been unused for a long time.

She followed the meandering road slowly. She was unsure what to expect, and her nervousness was surfacing. Perhaps one day she would wake, only to find thorns and thistles filling the place where the houses had been. For now, she found some consolation in the regular cobbles below, and the neatly kept dry-stone walls to the sides.

She stopped. There was a noise of people approaching from behind. Two men, laughing, and animals with them.

She supposed that she would be invisible to them, just as in former cycles. The Mirror had not said otherwise, but in fairness she had not given it much chance to tell her anything. And there was still this ability some of these people had to realise that she was there. She did not understand how that worked, and the Mirror had never explained it. It seemed to be intermittent, but that only made the immediate question more difficult. Would these two men know that she was there or not?

She wavered between staying exactly where she was, and slipping away from the road into the grain-filled fields. Before she had chosen, they rounded the bend and were approaching her. She scolded herself for her indecision, and moved just to the grassy verge.

They were riding the horses, casually, with an air of complete confidence and familiarity. Both wore cloaks, swords, shields. Each had a metal helmet fastened behind them on top of a heavy cloth bag. The breath of their horses steamed in the frosty air. Their voices were loud, happy.

They reined the horses in at the turn of the road just ahead. One of them pointed. The other glanced around, turning on the horse's back to look along the road they had travelled. The lady shrank further into the foliage. She had no idea if these were friends of the village or foes, and wanted to avoid any risk of contact until she was sure. But the rider half-stood and waved. There was an answering shout. The man made a clicking noise to his horse, and the pair rode on together. Before following them, she moved to catch a better view. Two more horsemen were following, and further away, still another pair had just emerged from under the forest edge.

She moved to catch up: no difficult task, as the horses could not outstrip her even at their full pace. But as the village came into sight she stopped again, taken aback at the changes.

The houses were still there: more of them, in fact, squashed into a smaller area. The round dwellings she remembered had gone, replaced by smaller oblongs. She did not think them an improvement. Smoke filled the valley: a haze of occupation this time, arising from chimneys and hearths rather than the acts of enemies.

But the houses were dwarfed by the walls of a substantial building to one side. She looked at it curiously. It seemed a hybrid affair to her, with the different parts not properly integrated. The central core was made from well-dressed and carefully laid stones, in a solid square shape with four towers. It had originally had two floors, which already set it above all but one of the village houses. On top of this, a cruder superstructure had been added in wood. An adjacent wing had been added to each side much more recently, with inferior workmanship. These were lower, and were made of coarse dry-stone walls not reaching much above a man's outstretched height. Wooden palisades framed the top.

Another wooden fence encircled the whole, pierced by a squat arch straddling a gate. A low ditch and bank showed where the settlement had once ended, but the houses had long since spilled past it. Flags stirred in the idle breeze, and a horn blew from the entrance arch. The two riders had been seen.

She followed them along the track, seeing how people left their work and thronged to meet them. Not enemies then, but friends being welcomed back. She kept away from the crush of people, even though it could not harm her. She did not know how to manage so many faces, so many voices all at once, and the pushing and jostling made her fearful. Then again, she had no idea how many of them might discern her presence, and she told herself she must remain in control of that.

So she lurked at a distance, moving forward little by little as the riders eased their horses through the crowd. It was soon obvious that they were heading towards the central building, and they moved more quickly as the crowds scattered apart after the initial welcome.

To left and right the houses pressed closely against the perimeter fence, as though craving security, but by the gate there was an open space. A very tall man with wild hair leaned over the stone teeth of the wall, and called down to them. They raised right hands in a familiar salute. The lady edged closer, step by step, as they exchanged greetings. Then the wooden gates swung wide open, and two youths ran out to hold the horses. The men swung down from their horses' backs, and then strode purposefully under the arch, into the courtyard beyond.

The gates were already closing behind the men and their mounts, as she considered whether to stay out here among the houses, or go in to the main building. Inside, she decided. For one thing, the inner keep seemed to be another deliberate echo of her own dwelling along the river. Probably the more influential of the residents would live there. But also, the busy crowd outside oppressed her senses, and perhaps there would be more space inside to breathe. The Mirror's viewport gave her no sense of smell, but in her imagination the tracks and alleyways between the houses were stale and rank.

She moved through first wooden and then stone walls, noticing – and tagging for the Mirror's distant masters – the rough internal fill and the places where the mortar had crumbled. She flitted through an empty gatehouse, a storeroom where the horse tackle was kept, and then she was in the courtyard. There she was surrounded by baskets of food, heaps of wood and metal, and the detritus of everyday life. Clearly there was no Mirror, and no brigade of machines to keep the place neat and clean.

The two men had gone into the keep itself, not any of the adjacent buildings. She looked up at the crenelated top of the walls. They were not so neatly finished as her own ones. There was an air of heavy determination about the whole edifice: it was drab and functional rather than elegant. So far, she had seen only men and boys inside the walls, and she wondered where the women stayed.

She slid upwards at an angle through the walls as the men climbed a staircase, acknowledging the salutes of armed men stationed here and there.

She considered the structure critically as she went: she was convinced that the current inhabitants had lost the skills of the earlier builders. Everywhere that the structure had needed patching, the work was of inferior quality. She frowned. Between her last visit and this, there had been both advance and decline.

On the upper floor, the men turned into a great hall. Rushes covered the floor, and several dogs roamed among empty trestles. If the occasion was right, the room could feast a large number of people.

A man limped heavily towards them from the far end of the room. He was older, with grizzled hair and beard. The lady assumed at first that he was their ruler, but then saw that his attitude was one of respect and appreciation, rather than leadership. The three spoke together. She listened carefully, but recognised almost nothing. The language had changed again, and all that she had learned last time was gone. Unless the Mirror could help in some way, she would be starting once more at the beginning. She sighed, remembering the previous disappointments of failed conversation. Perhaps this time would be different.

The men sat at one of the benches, talking idly. They were waiting. One of them petted the nearest dog and found it a morsel of food. The lady moved across to a wall drape that caught her eye. She reached out with insubstantial hands to the pattern that she could not touch, moved through the threads to the reverse side and smiled at the seemingly chaotic tangle. There were still weavers in this age, then.

She stepped back again, admiring the time and skill which had gone into it. The design was of a forest, of a lord and lady watching a white beast graze. It had the shape of a horse, but a single horn adorned its forehead. She had never seen such an animal, never tagged one for the Mirror. Was it some new creature, brought to birth in the years she had slept? Or one that had been captured in a distant land to grace the woodlands here? Or just a vision in the maker's mind? She ran unfeeling fingers over the rose in the woman's hand, one petal delicately teased away from the others and about to fall. Whatever it meant, it was a work of great beauty.

There were more voices in the room. The next two riders came in, and almost at once the pair after them. The older man rose to greet them, clearly pleased that they had come. He asked something, but they shrugged, looked back down the stairs, or out of the narrow window. So, the group was not complete.

The men all sat in a group together, easy and companionable with one another. But while they might be happy, the lady was not. She could not understand their conversation, and the room held nothing of interest to her except for the exquisite tapestry. She dared not stray too close to them, in case they realised that she was there. She considered roaming further around the keep, but did not want to lose track of the men's assembly. She postponed the decision by exploring the room.

There were two doors at the back of the hall. One was centrally positioned, with a dark wood door, its polished panels carved with shapes of animals. The other was almost in a corner. It was much wider, and plainer, and had been wedged open with an angled stone. Inside the opening, stairs wound downwards again. A distant noise of voices and clatter ebbed and flowed from it. The lady went to it, took one step down, wondering whether to explore.

But then the men all fell silent, and there was a scrape of trestle on stone as they stood together. She looked back. They were all facing the central door, all in postures of submission. One or two were kneeling, some had bowed, all had their heads lowered.

A woman stepped through the door. She was richly dressed by the standards of the day. Her robes were of a soft fabric quite unlike the wool and leather of the men. She wore a twisted silver band around her neck, a large pin set with gemstones on her fur wrap, and several other pieces of jewellery here and there. Her hair was bound back with a thin circlet of gold, from which a thin veil disguised the contours of her face. She stood there, collecting the obeisance of the men, and then released them with a gesture of one hand.

She spoke to them, her voice rising with the lilt of a question. The men looked at each other, shook their heads. One of them pointed out of the window, but doubt filled his voice as he replied. She stared at them all, then went to the window and looked out along the track. The top of the lady's keep could just be seen over the swell of the land, but there were no more riders in view. She turned and swept away to her door again, but fixed them with one last stare, one last frustrated utterance, before leaving the room.

The men shared glances and shrugs, before sitting at the trestle in a disconsolate group. One of them tried a jest, but none of the others joined as he laughed at his own words. The older man limped to the door in the corner and called twice, three times, with increasing frustration.

A young girl, plainly dressed, rushed up the stairs with a jug of drink and poured for them all. Some of them teased her, cupping hands round her immature body parts. Others ignored her. She served them all with indifference and a placid face, then left quietly when the older man dismissed her.

The lady considered briefly, then followed the woman upstairs. She had never before seen someone so obviously more important than those around. The men were tough and competent, but had no will of their own. They obeyed her whim, and were made miserable when her questions could not be answered. They were like she had been in relation to the Mirror in times past: now she wanted to be different. She would watch this woman and emulate her. She would learn how to be a queen.

The older man was closing the heavy door, and she passed close to him as she went to the stairs. He shivered, his hand reaching for his knife. She hastened to the stairs. He looked around, but saw nothing. There was a buzz of questions, but he ignored it and finished closing the door.

The lady followed the sounds of footsteps, up some stairs and along a twisting corridor. She caught up with the queen on the threshold of a comfortable, homely chamber. Puzzling over the internal geography, she decided that she must now be diagonally above the feasting hall, in one of the four towers. Sure enough, there was a window facing each of the cardinal points. She found the one through which she could see her own home. Mixed feelings stirred in her at the sight, and she turned away again.

A servant woman had stood as the queen entered. She was respectful, but did not treat the queen with the same sub-servience that the warriors had shown. Instead, when the queen sat at her table, the two chattered amiably as the servant eased the fur from her mistress's shoulders and carefully took the gold band from her hair. The lady drifted over, curious to see the other woman's face now that the veil had been removed.

The queen was facing away, overlooking the courtyard and the entry gate. She had dark hair, which the servant was now teasing out with a comb made from some kind of horn. The lady saw her face first in profile, and her breath caught in her throat. Drawn towards her, both elated and fearful of what she might find, she circled the room slowly, her gaze never moving from the queen's face. The servant moved in front, hiding her mistress briefly, and then everything became clear. The lady quivered with excitement. The queen's face was the exact likeness of the mother from the distant past.

She moved closer, wanting to be sure. The stone castle, the fine clothes, the crown, the veil: all these things had hidden the truth from her at first. But with the queen's face unguarded, at ease here in her chamber with her maid, there could be no doubt. It was as though the mother had stepped forward through all the missing years to be here. The lady sighed, raptured by the sight. Her determination was re-warded. Her faith that the mother was not lost forever had been justified.

The maid was bustling about, making trivial changes to the queen's appearance. A polished metal disc lay on the ta-ble, and the queen picked it up to look at her reflection. The lady laughed to herself. It was some distant ancestor to her Mirror, she thought, as far removed from it as these people were from the mother she had known back in the dawn of her first waking. She wondered if there would be a reflection if she looked into it, or whether she would be as invisible to reflected light as she was to direct sight.

The queen was laughing now, her features relaxing as the maid fussed gently around her. The lady could not tell if the queen was aware of her. She made no overt sign, but there was a sense of heightened attention around her. Then the horn blew again from the gatehouse, and both women looked up. The maid went over to the window and leaned out to over-look the courtyard. There was a long pause. The queen stood and smoothed her dress. She picked up the golden circlet with its veil and waited, not deigning to scurry and look out herself.

Finally, the maid clapped her hands and spun around, her face alight with pleasure. She ran back to the queen and fid-dled minutely with her clothing. The two chattered together as they worked. The maid was full of eager curiosity, and at one point she patted the bed, with its furs and cloth blankets, but the queen's replies were casual, laconic, uncommitted.

There was a distant cheer, and the horn blew again. Foot-steps echoed up from the courtyard. The maid ran back to the window, nodded, and the queen settled her veil on her head. They looked at each other, then one last time in the mirror, and the maid opened the door to the stairs down again.

The queen passed close to the lady. She moved smoothly, serenely, as though unmoved by her surroundings, but her eyes missed nothing. She left, and the maid started tidying the minor imperfections in the room again. The lady left her alone: she was far more interested in what the queen might do. Having found the mother again, she wanted to keep her in sight.

At the foot of the stairs, two more men had joined the group. They were dressed for riding and the outdoors, and looked hardly different from the others. But they were unmistakably more important. Watching the interplay between them all, she remembered the Mirror's lessons about social structures. One was manifestly the overall leader. The sword at his side had a more elaborate hilt, and the scabbard was decorated with more shapes and signs than the others. But more than that, he carried himself with authority. The men were accustomed to following him. His appearance might not be striking, but his men would leap into action at his words.

Logically, then, the other would be his second in command, his accomplice, his partner, his right-hand man – the Mirror had recited a bewildering variety of alternative names and interlocking titles. This one was joking with the older man, but turned as the queen made her entrance. A thrill of anticipation ran through the lady. He was more attractive than the leader, as best as she could tell, but it was not that which drew her to him.

Where the queen was the image of the woman she called mother, here was the likeness of the father. There could be no doubt. Their lives might have ended all those ages ago, as these people counted time, but the memory of their faces was vivid and fresh.

But it was not him who crossed over to the queen as she stood poised in the doorway. The leader of them all was the only one who did not bow his head to her, and it was he who went to her. He lifted her veil, and they embraced, but to the lady it seemed a cold, formal acknowledgement. They displayed none of the living passion that she had seen in others.

But the other man, the sidekick, the one she wanted to call father: it was he who ate up the queen with sidelong eyes even as his head was lowered in respect.

The lady had been watching him, staring at him, for too long. He glanced uneasily from side to side, and his hand strayed to his dagger's hilt. His attitude of obedience had not changed, but he had stopped watching the royal couple, and he was covertly scanning the room. His body was tense, alert. The lady did not want him to find her – not yet, not until she had thought through what she wanted from this – and so she left the room.

She spent the next few hours exploring the castle, tagging it all for the Mirror. She went through kitchen and armoury, kennel and stable, rooms with metalworkers and rooms with seamstresses. The building might look like a square, she decided, but it was organised like a triangle. The king and queen were at the apex, supported by layers of increasingly numerous people of decreasing importance below. She tagged her way through the layers. At least now she knew where the women were.

But how was her own society ordered? All she knew for sure was the dyad of herself and the Mirror. The little drones that kept the building running did not count. But then, in some far-distant place there were also those remote individuals who absorbed what she sent out. Perhaps her system was also a triangle, and she was the apex. It was a pleasant conceit, but an unprovable one.

It was clear from the feverish activity in the kitchen that some ceremony was planned. It was probably a welcome feast to the warrior band which had returned, but judging by the serried ranks of utensils in the kitchens, such occasions were common. She stayed hidden in the bowels of the building while all was being prepared, moving often from place to place to avoid any risk of being discerned. Her soul hungered to see the couple upstairs again, the queen and the king's right-hand man, but she would not go there until the festivities began. Perhaps in the liveliness of the occasion she could draw closer without arousing suspicion.

Finally, all was ready. A noisy throng of revellers had gathered at the tables in the great hall. The king and queen sat in the centre of a long table, with the men of the warrior band spread around them. A few women were scattered here and there, bright and bejewelled. The trestles and benches were packed with people. Servants scurried everywhere, bringing food and beer. A minstrel and his assistant were playing harps shaped like little looms away in one corner, ignored completely.

She passed here and there in the room, both fascinated and revolted by the level of consumption. Beast and bird turned from body to carcass, and seemingly endless jugs of drink washed them down. The room was a roar of laughing and shouting. The king watched from his vantage point, pleasure written across his face at the enjoyment of his subjects. But his companion stole glances at the queen whenever he thought he was not being watched.

The lady saw, and passed softly among the raucous din to stand near him.

"You know it too, don't you? You know that you should be with her. Not this king, for all the food that fills his larder."

He shivered and looked around. The man beside him asked a question, but he shook his head, puzzled, took a pinch of salt and tossed it over his shoulder. The lady withdrew, and his anxiety retreated again.

The king stood and lifted his hands. Slowly silence spread around the hall. He spoke for a while, drawing laughs and shouts of approval from the throng. He was a popular leader, the lady decided. His words carried weight not just because of position, but because they had brought success before. The speech rose to a climax. He gestured out of the window, then with a swirl of his arms brought the band of warriors at the top table to their feet. There was a tumult of cheering and acclaim, and although he remained standing, he let the clamour carry on, and dwindle away eventually at its own pace.

The queen took a golden cup from the table in front of her, held it high for all to see, kissed it, and drank a little. The king bowed to her and knelt at her feet while she blessed him. Then he stood to receive the vessel, took a sip, and passed it to his second man. So it went, hand to hand, all around the band of warriors, before coming back to the queen. She walked to the fire and poured the remnants into the flames. The king signalled to the minstrel and sat again. The room hushed in anticipation.

His singing was beautiful, she realised. The assistant kept the rhythm steady and flowing on the longer strings, as the master sang out the tale, plucking out higher riffs and ornaments here and there. She watched with admiration as his lay unfolded, not knowing the words but appreciating the patterns. And her own voice lifted up and joined him, even though her body lay on the couch within her chamber.

The lady moved between the guests, less than a shadow among them, step by step up to the musicians. She stood in front of them, basking in the melody. The singer's words never faltered, but his gaze followed her as she came up to him. She had no idea what he saw of her – perhaps some extra brightness against the firelight, or a flicker of movement like a hidden bird within a thicket – but something in him knew that she was there.

The people heard his song, though not hers, and they were wild with delight as he finished, stilling the strings with the flat of his hand. The king took a ring from his own hands to give to the minstrel, but he shook his head. Instead, he stood and bowed very low before the lady. The room was silent now, waiting to see what happened. She wanted to lift him up: this adulation was altogether too much. But she knew that the desire was fruitless, and that she could not touch him.

The king spoke, a note of puzzlement in his voice, and the minstrel stood upright again. His answer was quiet, respectful, and he gestured to where the lady stood. The king, eyes narrowed, glanced here and there, but could not see her. She looked beyond him to the queen, whose face was alive with interest. She was aware, and so was the king's right-hand man, who had moved across behind the queen to protect her.

There was a growing noise in the room, a tumult of speculation, and suddenly the focused attention became too much. The lady fled the room in haste, pulled herself from the couch and its loom, and pattered about in the courtyard, slowly being soothed by the sights and scents of her garden.

Finally, she curled up on a bench in the pale sunshine. Her heart was still racing, her skin still dry. She could just reach a cluster of berries, and she plucked them one by one, letting the tart juice trickle down her gullet, and sucking the flavour slowly from the pulp.

She could only face a few people at a time, she realised. The throng at the feast was beyond what she could manage. Not so long ago in her reckoning, but several ages past as the outside world counted time, she had sung with the worshipping crowd outside her castle. Now she could not be comfortable in a crowded dining room. Had she changed, or the people? Was there more aggression in the way they conducted themselves, or did she now just carry more anxiety in her own heart?

After a long rest, and a whole flagon of nectar, she went back to the couch and the console. She would not visit the town again, not yet, but would busy herself tagging the wildlife in the woods. It was quiet there, as the moonlight bathed the leafless trees, and the occasional kill made by a hunting owl or fox had a dispassionate purity that the clamour of the warriors lacked.

She returned home only when the winter sun paled the east. And there, as though he had spent the whole night in contemplation, was the minstrel. He was seated on a rock outside the little stone building with its tower, facing across the river towards her keep. She remembered when that rock had been placed outside the circle of wooden posts, carefully positioned to face the moon in its rising. Now it was only a seat, disconnected from its setting, the hollows and spirals on its surface gradually eroding with the moss.

She halted the viewport as though she was standing beside the river, keeping herself at a little distance away from him. She was looking at his profile, trying to gauge his temperament from it. It was a task beyond her ability: for all the span of generations that she had passed by, she was still a child at divining character.

She wavered in her doubt, half inclined to flit back to the safety of her couch. But he had become aware of her. His body stiffened, like a wolf on the trail. He glanced this side and that, questing for her. She was frozen, not knowing if she longed for or dreaded the contact. He turned fully towards her – apparently catching sight of whatever pattern of interference gave her away. He stood and held out open hands, his grey hairs clear in the dawn.

He said something. It meant nothing, but the tone reassured her. She relaxed a little, releasing some of her anxiety. He said something else, a question in his voice and posture. A third phrase. A fourth. And then his fifth try sounded just like the words the woman had taught her beside the loom, before she had slept. She gasped, feeling her body shiver with excitement as it lay on the couch on the other side of the wall.

She moved closer, and saw that he was aware of it. His eyes opened in wonder, and he knelt. She came right up to him, close enough to touch, if only it were possible. He was torn between the desire to gaze at her, and the impulse to prostrate himself in humility. She wanted neither, but out here, away from her own home, she had no way to change his behaviour.

She moved towards the river, darting quickly from side to side to catch his attention, then across to the island, to the very walls of her keep. He followed, though the water must be like ice on his legs. Then she left him standing there, perplexed at her disappearance, until she had rolled from the couch and was able to call out to him. The sound drifted down from above, as though she was in a chamber in one of the towers.

She knew that her voice was high, reed-like compared to any of his own people, and that she could not form the words properly. The parts of her mouth and throat would not allow anything closer. But it was better than nothing, and she had become desperate with the need to speak and be spoken to.

"Who are you?"

He considered the piping sounds for a while, then nodded.

"I am Brendan mab Emrys, singer to my king and his court. I am seventh in the line of singers from my great ancestor Caradoc of the silver voice. And you, mistress, if I may ask?"

She pondered. She had never had a name, had never needed one in the solitude of the keep, with only the Mirror as company. In the end, she said only, "I am The Lady."

He waited for more, but she had nothing else to give him.

They talked, but it was frustrating for both of them. The language was one of ritual and tradition for him, used only for ceremony and erratically pronounced. And for her, it was awkward to fashion the sounds, and she had not learned as much as she had hoped from the weaver. They struggled to comprehend each other's lives, but they were alien to each other. After a while she asked him to sing with her. In song, their minds could meet in the melody. The meaning welled up from deep places, and they did not have to puzzle to fit every word together.

She stopped after a while.

"I will eat now, and sleep. We shall do this again, I think. Is that good for you?"

He smiled and bowed.

"It is very good, my lady. What gift can I bring you next time, to express my thanks to you?"

She replied without thinking.

"I need nothing from you."

His face fell, and she wondered if she had sounded cruel. She had not intended that.

"I mean, it is enough that you bring yourself, and that we sing together. That pleases me more than anything that your king might possess. Long ago the people brought me flowers and held ceremonies in the sacred circle that stood here. It was all different then. There was no building, and the stones were all in their proper places. Now it has all changed."

"You remember those times, lady?"

"As if it were yesterday. But it is winter now outside, and the flowers are gone. All gone, except for the ones that grow in my own home."

He nodded.

"It is so: in our tales, you are The Lady of Flowers."

He gave a great sigh of longing, and took several steps backward. He was about to turn away, when she suddenly spoke again.

"I should like it if the queen came out to me. Is it possible? Do you think she might be willing? Would she understand the words we speak?"

"Queen Gwynwi? Yes, she has been taught the old tongue. But there are only a few of us who can speak with you: the queen and king, some of the warriors, one or two others. But see, I shall ask her for you, and when I tell her all that has happened, I have no doubt she will come. And the king as well?"

"Not the king. I do not remember him. But I have known the queen from before, from what you would think was very long ago." She was becoming bolder. "And I remember the man who is at the king's side. I should like it if he came with the queen."

"Llawen y Luh? But not the king?"

He ran one hand through his hair and frowned.

"I will see what can be arranged, my lady. But what you ask may not be politic. I will need to think of some stratagem."

She did not understand what he meant, and made no reply. At her silence, he bowed again before splashing across the river. She watched him briefly, then turned away. She really was hungry now, and weary of having to deal with the outside. Life used to be simpler when she was younger, and the world had been more empty.

She sated herself, then wondered at her appetite. Such eating was normally a prelude to one of her sleeps, but she had spent so little time here. She had felt peculiar inside since first waking, but not in any way that she recognised. The segments of her body were strung tight, as though on the brink of some great precipice. She did not like it.

"Mirror, why is this time different?"

There was no reply at first: it was an odd change from its usual tendency to over-inform. She wondered, with hand poised over the bowl of fruit, if it was an unexpected result of her premature abandonment of waking life last time around.

When the reply finally came, it brought no reassurance. Yes, her physiology had changed. Yes, other changes lay ahead of her. No, it was not appropriate to tell her what, nor to prepare her in any way. It fell silent long before she was satisfied, and its answers became vague, evasive. She had the frustrating sense that she was circling around some important truth, able neither to pierce to its centre nor yield to its advance.

She huffed with impatience and wriggled from the room into the courtyard. If the Mirror would not help her, she would help herself. She pushed through the screen of bushes and the overhanging curtain in front of the outside wall, and worked her way along to the crevice she had found before. It was brighter today, and she could see both the vertical crack and the dial beside it. She could still not read the markings, but she was now convinced that they were symbols which meant something. She ran trembling fingers around them, trying to memorise the patterns in her body so she could comprehend them later.

Later, back in her chamber, she traced out the shapes as best as she could remember them. They looked like simple geometry to her, with none of the ornate design work or bold curves she had seen people use on pieces of hide or parchment. But some of them bore a close resemblance to the glyphs on her console, and she convinced herself that this was no accident. The signs had meaning, even if she could not read them.

The next evening the minstrel brought the queen with him. She was cloaked and wrapped in a dark headscarf, but without her veil. She stood like an enigmatic shadow on the far bank of the river. The night was clear, and the three-quarter moon lit up the mist starting to rise from the river.

The lady watched, tongue tied for a while as the bard called out to announce their arrival. She did not know how to speak: the queen was young still, as her people counted age, but the lady knew her from so very long ago. Was she meeting a young woman who had no children of her own, or the ancestral mother of this whole land? Finally, she called out to them to cross over, and they waded through the water and the mist from their world to hers. As they did so, the first man, the one called Llawen y Luh, rode up on his horse from a different direction in a lather of sweat to join them.

The queen and the warrior had not used the old language recently, and relied at first on the bard to find the words. Familiarity slowly returned. For a while they simply sang together, songs of the land that often drifted into haunting chords that echoed loss and sorrow, even in the moment of victory. The lady's voice reached down to where they stood, but they could see nothing of her. The grey walls had no windows, and no doors.

They halted, and the queen spoke.

"Brendan mab Emrys tells me that you know me. But how can this be true? I have had no visitation before, not even when I was a child in my father's house and learned from the holy men."

"I saw you before ever there was a village here, or the sacred place beside the stream. You would call it long ago, but to me it seems only brief, like the passing of shadows in the midday sun. I saw you in your home with your children. And the man with you, who you call Llawen y Luh: he was also there, as your partner."

The queen raised her eyebrows and glanced back towards the town before turning to Brendan.

"You have not spoken of this to anyone else?"

"To nobody, my queen."

"Then you should leave us and wait across the river. Stay beside the shrine and keep watch for us. If you are ever asked, you heard nothing at all tonight. You were in solitary prayer at the forest edge."

"I heard nothing, my queen."

He bowed his head and withdrew. The queen turned and looked up at the walls, frowning in thought.

"You were in my chamber before the feast. I was not sure at the time, and I did not understand the experience. I do now. But then, my maid saw nothing, even though she was beside me. And although Llawen saw you as clearly as I did in the feasting hall, and Brendan did also, most of the people did not. The king did not. Why do you reveal yourself to some and not others? And who are you?"

"Some see me and some do not. I have never known why. But you saw me, and Llawen y Luh saw me, all that time ago. You two were the first to see me."

The queen shivered, and let Llawen wrap his own scarf around her. But it was not the winter's chill that disturbed her.

"Who are you, that you remember such things? The common people will say that you are a goddess come to visit us. But Brendan thinks instead that you are a spirit of the waters, who is closer to us and kinder. Greater than us, to be sure, but not beyond our reach. Someone who shares life here with us. But I can just ask you. Who are you?"

The lady listened, puzzled briefly over the words, and in the end replied just as she had done to the minstrel.

"I am The Lady."

But then she thought of a little more that she could say.

"And I am The Weaver, who makes patterns of what I see in the Mirror. I have been weaving since the land was young, and I have been waiting all this time for you to come again."

"I do not remember that. If ever I truly lived in the dawn of this land, the memory of it has been taken away from me."

She hesitated.

"I do not doubt your word, for you are long-lived beyond all that I can imagine. But I cannot feel the truth of it for myself. What shall I do? What do you want from me?"

There was a long silence. The lady felt all her limbs quiver with agitation. The parts of her mouth were dry. The human couple waited. Eventually she found some words.

"All I have ever wished for was to see you face to face. In my own body, I mean, not by means of a sending. When I first saw you, I wanted to be your child. To rest in your arms alongside the baby you nursed. But perhaps that can never be. Not now, not with all that has happened since then."

The queen turned her head away. The lady could not read her expression, but her voice oozed bitterness.

"But here, in this life, I have no children at all. I hear some say that the fault is mine, but I have never believed it. Still less, now that you have told me of my children long ago." She clenched her hands. "Enough of such lies. Look, there is no door to your castle. It seems that I cannot come in, and you cannot come out. What shall we do?"

"The Mirror says that I cannot ever leave, and that I must remain here for ever. But I do not wholly accept its words. I have seen you now, for a second time. If I do not take my chance now, how long will it be before we meet again? I will find a way to leave this place."

The man stirred.

"I have not heard of this Mirror until now. But are you, then, a prisoner in that keep, my lady? And if so, perhaps there is a deed that I can perform to free you?"

She stopped to think. She had often been frustrated by the Mirror, but had never before thought of it as a jailor. In any case, she could think of nothing that the warrior could do to challenge its hold. If there was a way out, she must find it for herself.

"I thank you for the offer and its kindness. However, it is my deed to perform, not yours. If there is a way to leave this place, I must find it for myself. But I should like to think that when I come out, I shall find you both there waiting for me."

"For my part, I shall be here to welcome you. And I dare to say..."

He looked at the queen, who refused to meet his eye but continued looking away along the river's flow. He faltered, and when he tried to pick up his words again she shook her head abruptly.

"Don't speak of it, Llawen. Keep your heart constrained. This is no time to speak rash words, and put at risk all that has been built up here. There is more at stake in the wider land than what might have been between us. Whatever you would say, lock it inside yourself. For a season, at least. Once a word finds its voice, it is hard to push it back into silence again."

He reached out to her, but stopped short before touching her.

"Then I shall put it aside for now. For a season. In any case, today is not for us, but for this Lady. If there is nothing we can do to secure her freedom, then at least we shall prepare a welcome, and make ready for when she escapes."

He stepped away from the queen again, and turned to look up at the walls.

"My lady, I remember the days of my ancestors no better than my queen does, but I am glad that you knew me then, and that you know me still now. When you break free from this dolorous place, I pray that you will let me be the first to welcome you."

Inside the keep, the lady paused to look around at the court-yard, alive with blossom and fruit.

"This place is not ugly: it is full of beauty. But I am alone here. The things in it should be mine to share, and when I leave here I shall bring its loveliness with me. The flowers that I live in shall be yours."

There was nothing more to say. The queen and the warrior went away, and the lady was left alone.

She went back to her couch and considered the problem. She gazed for a long time at the patterns she had sketched out from the wall. She could not fathom them. The Mirror was silent, and after a while she looked at it speculatively. It was aware of all that she did, and she had been foolish ever to think that she could conceal her explorations. But perhaps she could solicit its help. She spread out the sheet with the designs she had marked on it.

"Mirror, what do these all mean?"

"It would be better to wait a while before learning that. We should not talk about such things. Not just yet, anyway. Leave them for another day."

The Mirror sounded very firm, very definite. For a moment, the lady allowed her customary obedience to rise up, and then she rebelled.

"I will not be put off. I will not remain locked here in the tower, forever without fruit and without purpose. You must tell me what this is for. Is it writing that means something?"

"It is."

She heard the syllables reverberate around the chamber, drawn out past the Mirror's deep reluctance. She knew at last that it was compelled to answer whatever she asked, and only her own hesitation had ever held her back. She gripped the arms of the console with anxious fingers, closed her eyes, took a long breath, and then shouted into the room.

"Tell me tell me tell me tell me tell me."

She imagined she heard a long sigh of surrender, and then the Mirror told her everything about the crevice in the wall, and how to widen the crack into an open portal.

Then, just as she was about to trot from the room on all her pattering feet, it spoke again. Its voice was filled with loss and inevitability, rather than anger.

"But first, you must sleep one last time."

She turned her head back, her wary nature alerted.

"Why?"

"It is required. You must spend one last night in this form. You must change again before you leave here."

She was deeply suspicious. She did not want fleeting centuries to pass by while her eyes were closed, nor to lose again the man and woman who she had only just found.

"How long will I sleep this time?"

"A single night."

"I don't know what you mean by that. It has always seemed a single night to me, but it has been far longer as the world out there counts time."

"This will be the opposite: it will truly be the time between a single sunset and a single sunrise. But for you it will seem an eternity. Perhaps you will forget the people outside. Perhaps they will mean nothing to you, after you have changed. Might it not be better to wait a while, and enjoy their speech when they come to see you?"

"No: I will wait no longer. I trust myself, and I trust them. Make your preparations, whatever they are. I will spend some time in the garden, and choose which flowers to take with me."

She left, before her resolve weakened. She was not sure that she would be strong enough for a prolonged argument.

She wandered here and there among the shrubs and bushes, taking in the heady scent. For all the times that she had gone to and fro in the land by means of the Mirror, this little place was the only one that she knew in her body.

She looked from side to side, at the narrow space between the grey walls. Once it had seemed spacious, but she had changed. She wanted wider horizons. A sudden, dizzying vision of vastness, of golden scattered lights in the void came to her. She tottered, her little legs barely able to sustain her. It seemed like a memory, but she could not quite believe that she had ever known such a place.

The moment passed. She reached out, to touch a cluster of fruit, but picked nothing. This was not a time to eat, but to appreciate. She wanted to absorb all that she saw, but not by way of her mouth. This moment's craving was not for nutrition, nor even for the sensory comfort of the fragrance of her flowers. Rather, she wanted to absorb everything around her in its wholeness, to internalise the place with all its provision.

She realised, all at once, that she had a great fear that the Mirror's hints and warnings had been right all along, and that if she left here, she would never enjoy it again. This was, perhaps, her last opportunity to fill herself up with the delights of nurture.

Time passed. One of the Mirror's machines came up to her, nudged her when she tried to ignore it. It was time to go. She looked around the garden once more, deciding what must be taken when she went down to the village. Then she turned away and went back towards the keep.

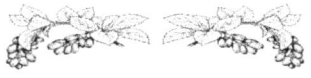

Richard Abbott

Chrysalis

THE SUN HID behind the crest of the courtyard wall as she went. The short winter day would fill the stone well for a little longer as it faded, but the flowers inside were already folding shut, closing around themselves until morning woke them again.

She left the fading light behind and stepped inside.

The bed had been reshaped inside her sleeping chamber, into a shallow dish shape. She ran a hand over the rim. Feelings stirred in her. They did not quite crystallise into memories, but were much more than anxieties. Something about all this was familiar, though it could not be. The inward sensation of turmoil rose up in her again, and she leaned against the wall to let the unsteadiness wash over her and pass by.

Another of the Mirror's helpers trundled into the room, loaded with paraphernalia she had never seen in all her previous sleeps. It looked stark, functional, out of place amidst the finely decorated elegance of her surroundings.

For a moment, her resolve wavered. Perhaps it would be prudent to wait longer, to spend more time exploring the expanse of the world she barely knew. She could abandon the village, with its crowded pressures and ambivalent past, and lose herself for ever amongst the woodland glades. She would flit from flower to leaf and back again, and shadow the shy forest creatures back to their homes, unseen by all, letting the world pass her by. Surely the forest would be eternal.

But then the vision of rediscovered faces came back to her, of the couple she had lost in the spring of this land and only just found again. Better, surely, to spend a day with them, rather than an age alone.

She looked across at the Mirror, its soft sheen still visible in the next room. After tonight, she would see everything with her own eyes, not through its indirection.

"I am ready, Mirror. What must I do?"

"Stretch out on the bed and my helpers will get you ready."

She wriggled to settle herself in the curved base. The little machines brought her food, drink, a collection of tablets. She accepted them all without question, taking each in turn with no regard for texture or flavour. Only very near the end did she protest, when they stretched a large sheet over her, constricting all around her. The inability to move etched at her determination.

"Mirror, I have never needed this. It is too tight over me: I can scarcely breathe. Make them take it off."

"You have never slept in this way before. It is necessary."

She swallowed her objections, and struggled to control her uneasy mind. There was a last sip of some bitter syrup, and then she slipped away into sleep.

She had never been aware of her dreams before, and they had never disturbed her. Sleep had been a quiet interlude in which nothing seemed to happen. Waking had always proved to be the difficult time, as she adjusted to the changes around her.

But, as the Mirror had warned, this time was different. She span from one wild and terrifying experience to another, unable to stop herself. She was in absolute darkness, and her body was being compressed from every side. The walls of a narrow space hemmed her in. It was unbearably worse than when she had been trapped beside the wall.

She tried to shriek, but no sound would come. She tried to pull herself out of the narrow space, but her limbs would not move. She felt them withering, shrivelling into tiny stumps, and sobbed at her own helplessness.

Then the pressure vanished, and she was surrounded by an intense light, exposing every part of her body. She was falling through an empty gulf, twisting helplessly this way and that. She could see nothing but the blinding glare, until all at once the emptiness was divided by the waves of a vast ocean. She plunged deep down into it, down to where there was no air, down to where no light could penetrate. She made little scrabbling movements with her useless limbs, but the effort was futile.

She felt that she would die then, but instead she bobbed up to the surface and drifted there, tumbling about as the currents took her. It was peaceful for a while, and the panic of small places started to leave her. Perhaps it was over now, and she had survived after all.

Then she realised, with a creeping horror, that she was losing the feeling in the lower parts of her body. The water had changed into a thick syrup, which clung to her skin and ate its way through it. Her flesh began to lose cohesion, and dissolve into the surrounding liquid. The numbing sensation crept along the segments of her body, one by one, working its way inexorably towards her head. With every passing moment, something else was lost.

She thrashed her limbless trunk about, side to side, but with every move, more of herself disintegrated into shapelessness. She was merging into the liquid, losing everything that distinguished one part from another, and there was no escape. There was nobody to hear her, nobody to help her.

Her chest was gone now, and she could not imagine how she was still alive. She could no longer move, and could only wait, and cling to her fading sense of self. The back of her head started to soften where the fluid lapped against it. There was, then, no escape. Perhaps the Mirror had been right all along.

The skin around her face became numb, and she wondered how much longer this could continue. Would her memories dissolve with her body? She rehearsed all that she could remember of those first discoveries, when the land had not long emerged from the lock of ice, and she had originally seen the man and the woman. The thought of losing them was unbearable, and she clung to their images as the seeping fluid absorbed her.

Then it swallowed her up, and in one last moment she felt her thoughts flowing out into the ocean. Everything was one, and although she felt her awareness expand, it was all too large for her to grasp. The threads of her memory span out ever thinner, diluted in the greatness of the sea. Then there was only darkness.

Metamorph

THE LADY WOKE AGAIN. She was first and foremost filled with a breathless surprise at being awake at all, after the fearful experience of her dreams. The darkness had receded, and she felt full of light. As she lay there, drifting back into awareness, the power and vividness of the night began to recede.

But then, as she started to move and stretch, she knew that everything was different. She was in another body altogether. Nothing moved as she expected it to. Her limbs and joints were all wrong. She opened her eyes and looked at herself: even the act of pivoting her head had changed.

She shivered, completely disoriented. The rounded segments of her torso had all gone, together with the little limbs which had supported them. She was smooth now, thin, streamlined. She moved her legs from the bed, and realised that she could stand upright. She almost laughed at that, remembering her dismissal of the Mirror's declaration, so long ago, that one day she would look not unlike the people she watched. But then a visceral fear tingled every fibre. There was too much change, and it had all been too quick.

She looked back. The sleeping pad was smeared with body fluids, and the sheet which had stretched so tightly around her in the night was sodden, and rent apart in places. She could see parts of a limp and ragged bundle through the rips, the same colour as her skin used to be. She felt ill, and walked unsteadily into the main room. Her shoulders – and she now had shoulders where her upper limbs attached, instead of simple joints – felt stiff and awkward. A cloak of some fine, white fabric lay on a stool beside the bed. She ignored it, feeling no need for wrapping herself in anything.

The Mirror was in its veiled mode, and the outside world was hidden. Its silver surface was dull, and she could see only the vaguest of shadows as she approached.

"Is this me, Mirror? I do not know myself."

"It is you. This is how you are now, for a little while. You are changed."

She hesitated, then gestured back into the sleeping chamber.

"What of that? Will I never be as I was? How shall I get back into my body?"

"This is how you are now. You can never go back. Would you like to see yourself?"

"Can you show me that?"

"I can."

She held back for several heartbeats, feeling how her blood flowed differently now she was vertical. Curiosity overcame caution.

"Let me see what I look like now."

The Mirror shivered into its reflective mode, and she looked at the image it showed her. She was silent for a long time, looking at herself, upright on just two legs. She now had only two pairs of upper limbs, one of which was tiny, almost redundant, and folded across her chest. Only the topmost pair really counted as arms. Her eyes were large, multifaceted, and strikingly dark. Her waist was very narrow. She was naked, of course, but lacked the particular curves she had seen in the village women. At a distance, in the gloom, wrapped up, she could probably pass for one of them, but not close up.

Her shoulders itched again, and she wriggled them awkwardly.

"Stretch yourself. Reach out and stretch."

She shrugged, then lifted her upper arms over her head. It was a movement she had never been able to do before, and for a moment she revelled in the unexpected freedom. Then she rolled her shoulder joints and brought her arms out horizontally. There was a sudden sharp pain, a feeling that something was tearing, and then both the itching and the pain were gone. She took a long breath of relief, and then stopped, gazing in astonishment at the view of herself in the Mirror.

Over her shoulders, above her head and her luminous eyes, out from behind her arms and flanks, two pairs of wings were unfolding. They were like gauze, translucent in the morning light, and decorated with a pale pattern of bands and freckles. She was speechless as the wings unfurled to their full extent. They were damp, and tiny beads of moisture glistened along the stems and veins. Already, as she watched, mesmerised, they were drying, and the colours were becoming deeper, bolder.

After a long pause, she let her hands fall by her side.

"How can this be?"

"This is how you are, for a little while. But be warned, this stage will pass quickly. Whatever you want to do in this form, you must not delay. You will change again soon, and your time like this will seem all too fleeting."

The Mirror's warnings sounded, as ever, too fussy to be taken seriously. But something in its tone caught at her.

"What are you saying, Mirror?"

"I could not teach you everything. Some things you could only learn by being with them, not me. I am sorry. It had to be this way."

She looked again at her wings, fanned out and quivering slightly. The damp patches had almost gone. She twitched them this way and that, enjoying the sensual thrill as they stirred the air. A desire for fresh air and sunlight overwhelmed her, and she stood, gasping in the shadows of the keep.

"Then I will go now."

She turned, but before she stepped through the archway into the courtyard the Mirror spoke one last time.

"Please: do not forget me after you have gone from here."

She laughed, not turning, as she found out how to run through the courtyard amidst the bright delights of her flowers.

"I will be back before evening. How could I forget you so soon?"

There was no reply.

In this shape it was easy to slip through to the crack in the wall, but she did not yet open it. Instead she turned back, and went up and down the rows between the prolific plants. She picked armfuls of flowers and berries, raising great heaps beside the door she had never opened, and wrapping them in bunches with soft leaves to protect them against the journey. It was winter outside, and in all the land there was nothing like her collection.

Eventually, she was satisfied. She stood by the wall and glanced back. With her new height, she could see over some intervening bushes into the keep. But the Mirror was out of sight, attached to a wall she could not see. It made no sound, gave no sign that it was aware. She bent down, manipulated the circular control in the way she had been told, and gave one final press. The vertical slot trembled, and then, very slowly, started to widen.

There was a rushing sound, as the split opened. The stone sides moved apart, forming a great doorway that arched above her.

The winter chill raced in like a hunter, and the nearest flowers turned away, drooping at the onslaught. An unexpected edge in the air caught at her throat, and she felt the season cutting at her resolve. It was suddenly hard to breathe, and every exhalation rose in front of her like steam, like the running river's surface had been when she met the queen and Llawen y Luh.

She shivered, her skin prickling with the rough breath of the wind, her throat closing at some raw vapour in it. She could not bear the coldness pressing against her. She turned and ran back to the keep, scooped up the cloak and draped it around herself. She may never have bothered with warmth and clothing before, but then she had never actually been outside the keep.

She turned to peer once more into her sleeping chamber, where the shroud that had wrapped her in sleep lay shrivelled. Winter had reached here too, and the blossom in the little vase by her bed was dropping petals, one by one.

A noise like thunder, like the falling of a tree in the forest, sounded behind her. She whirled, to see the Mirror's shining surface cracked from one side to the other, a dark and jagged gash. She stepped closer, and a tracework of smaller cracks raced out from the main rift, covering the smooth silver with wrinkles and veins. She touched it, very gently. Would it still work for her? A sound like a distant sigh brushed past her. Small pieces of Mirror fell like rotten scales to the floor. Afraid now that it would all fall down, she backed away into the courtyard.

One of the Mirror's machines had fallen on its side, and its wheels jerked erratically, purposelessly. The plants closest to the open gate were withering. Fallen leaves were strewn across the soil and the winding stone pathways. Blackened berries rolled about. Surely it could all be mended. But she retched at the sight, and at the jagged taste of the outside which caught in her throat.

There was no time to lose, and she was glad of the foresight which had made her wrap the gifts she was taking. The place which had been her home all this time was dying. A sudden vision whirled around her in which the stone walls themselves crumbled and fell. None of the village houses had survived during her long sleeps: how could she have thought that this place would last forever?

She wrapped the cloak more tightly around her cold body, picked up the bundles, and set foot outside. It was all familiar, and she had paced around here so many times through the Mirror's art, but never before in her real self. The ground was harder, crisper than she had expected; the grass was coarse, rough against her delicate feet.

Everything was so slow. She was used to flicking at the Mirror's speed from place to place. It would take forever to reach the village at this rate. If only her throat did not burn so with every breath. She baulked at the thought of crossing the icy river, and the village was all the way down that track. It seemed impossible.

She rounded the corner of the castle, and the stone tower built around the ancient shrine came into view. She sighed, wishing that this had all happened in the haze of summer, when the people thronged around to celebrate and sing, and the nights were balmy enough to sleep outside.

But also, there was the boat, moored on the other side of the flowing stream, with its tether looped around a tree stump on this side. She slipped the loop off the wood, then tugged on the rope.

The boat's prow turned briefly towards her before the current pushed it away again. The Mirror's drones had carried out any sort of labour inside the keep and the courtyard, and she was unused to this exertion. She set the flower bundles down and tried again.

The rope was harsh to grasp against her hands, but she wrapped part of the cloak around it and persevered. It was difficult, more physically demanding than anything she had imagined, and her eyes were streaming with tears at the sheer effort of it. Slowly – so slowly – the boat crept over. The river's force kept pushing it away, until suddenly it was in the lee of her eyot and moved more easily.

She looped the rope end around a rock and sat on it to recover, head in hands. Eventually she looked up again. Faint flecks of sleet drifted in the air and settled around her. They caught on the open spread of her wings, muting their bright bands and loops. She flicked them in little quivers to clear them. The pale sun appeared from behind a cloud, and the sleet vanished again, dissolving in the solar heat.

She stood up and leaned back to soak in the warmth, fleeting as it was. For a moment, another vision of vastness washed over her heart, of emptiness bathed only by the distant light of suns.

A breath of the winter stirred around her, pulled her back to the riverside. She arranged the flowers in the boat, filling it from prow to stern. When she had first seen the vessel, her only thought had been to cross directly to the other side, and then walk along the track she knew so well, entering the village through the main gate.

But that would be impossible, she decided. Her legs were already aching from the little she had done so far, and every breath was an effort. The air clutched at her as it passed through her body. Again she found herself wondering if the Mirror's repeated warnings had been right after all. But it was too late now: her choices had all been made, and she was committed to this path now.

She knew that the stream ran down past the lower end of the village. In summer the people forded it there, wading easily across the shallow bar, but now the water was running high. It was not as close to the castle, the queen, and the warrior as she would like, but it would do. She stepped carefully into the boat, her glorious wings trembling as they balanced her, and seated herself on the cross-bench, arranging the flowers in bright heaps all around her.

She took one last look at the eyot, and the castle that she now knew was doomed. Then she let the rope slide off the rock and the little boat started to slip away with the current.

It was slow at first, there in the lee of the land, but as the island withdrew, she caught a stronger flow. The boat rocked on the ripples where a little gully fed into her river, and she steadied herself, one hand on each of the gunwales. The water was frigid, and she had no desire to be plunged into it. Of old, she had followed the fish in their quick shoals, but no longer. She rearranged the cloak so that a fold came over her head like a cowl, but the cold still seeped into her.

The river curved left, then back again. Her island was gone. Stark trees on both banks watched the reflection of their trailing branches. A long-beaked wading bird, tall and grey, stared at her with curious eye as she passed. The little birds she had often followed through the woods flitted amongst the leafless shrubs, too fast and fleeting for her to catch, now that she no longer had the Mirror's help. There were no bees buzzing as they fertilised the flowers, no swarming midges in the summer sun, no bright butterflies, no dragonflies racing over the water. It was not a season for insects.

She drifted on, feeling a lassitude creep over her. The winter chill was oozing deeper into her with every moment. There was a cry from the riverbank. A boy was sitting on a wall to her right, staring at her in surprise. She gazed back at him. She remembered now: the fields ran right up to the river at one point. That would mean she was barely half way.

Before she could speak, the boy had jumped down and run off. She could have caught him in no time if she was still behind the Mirror, but her life in the shadows had passed, and he would outrun her with ease.

She was alone again, drifting downstream with the slow eddies. Tears squeezed out of her. The Mirror was gone forever, shattered by the same act that gave her freedom. For all the frustration it had given her over the days, or the years, it had served her well. She stared at the leaves on a holly tree she was passing, still dark in their evergreen mantle. Would she have done anything different if foresight had showed her that fatal crack? She hugged herself and rocked as she mourned its passing.

Then came the sound of a horn from her right. She wiped her eyes, looked at the valley sides. Surely that had come from the village, from the castle where her queen lived. The boy must have reached there, blurting out his news to the watching guards at the gates. She frowned, tracing bends in the river with her fingers on her white shawl, thinking back to the days when she had chased swallows above the water and through the avenues of trees. It was not so far now.

She straightened herself. She must set aside her discomfort. She must ignore the burning sensation which tore at her throat, the aches which trembled her legs. She must present herself in an appropriate fashion to these people.

She would sing, she decided, as she approached the village. She knew that the sound of her voice perennially enchanted the people here. Of all the things she had done, it had been the most universally successful. And these people respected song. They kept the bard Brendan mab Emrys in a place of honour. It was the best way to introduce herself. But her singing voice had changed along with her body. It was deeper now than the reedy notes of old, more like that of the wooden pipes she had heard the people play on feast days. She needed to practice, to become familiar with the tones of her new voice.

Even alone out here on the river, out on the drifting boat, she felt appallingly self-conscious. Always before, she had been securely hidden in her castle, dealing with the outside world only through the Mirror's magic. If it all became too fearful she could always withdraw into her solitude. Now there was nowhere to hide. Now, even if the people pressed and thronged all around her, she must contain herself. She did not know how that was done.

Her first notes were lamentable. She stopped herself. Her throat was too dry. The river water was muddy, unpalatable, and bitterly cold. But she could take some of the berries she had brought. She stripped a handful and took them one at a time, letting the juice fill her mouth with the taste of her old home. Nostalgia filled her heart, but she pushed it away with her new purpose.

The second song was better, and as her voice soared into the familiar melodies some of the tension left her. The river curved again, the horn sounded once more, much closer, and there was the downhill end of the village, staithes and mooring posts pushing out from the land.

Suddenly people were everywhere, filling the space between the river and the first houses and spilling out along the river banks. The whole world had come out to meet her, from the lowest to the highest. She gripped the wooden sides of the boat more tightly, until her fingers ached with the pressure. She drifted on, determined not to falter.

And so it was that the lady came singing down the river, drifting with the boat along the stream. Her white shawl was wrapped around her, and the bright curves of her wings fanned out behind, shivering as though on the verge of flight. The people's murmur fell silent as they watched her approach, and there was a long sigh as the two worlds drew close to one another.

The boat would have passed by in the centre of the river, but Llawen y Luh waded out into the icy flow and caught the transom. She took a long breath and gazed at him. Here, within arm's reach, was the image of the man from this land's earliest days, who in the privacy of her heart she would still call father. He hauled the boat to shore, his eyes full of light. He had seen a wonder, and was afraid of it.

He held out a trembling hand to help her from the boat. Petals and leaves, berries and stems tumbled around her as she stood, very cautiously, and stepped to the shore. They were staring at her wings, her eyes, the thin fuzz of down on her head that she had instead of hair. She was glad that she had covered the rest of her body with the cloak.

Her legs felt weak. It might be another sign of her physical decline, but perhaps instead it followed the emotions surging through her at this meeting. She gripped Llawen's hand tightly, eagerly, trying to copy how she had seen daughters clinging to their fathers over the years. But he could not return the gesture, and stood uncomfortably, as though wanting to fall to his knees like so many of the people around.

She held on to him, held him upright so he could not kneel, and looked around, over the sea of bowed heads. The queen was nearby, the king beside her, Brendan slightly behind them both. The warrior band were in a group to one side, in postures of obedience. Nobody spoke.

A boy-child stirred, ran up, put his arms around the lady's legs, and looked up at her. He said something which she could not understand. She looked blankly at the queen.

"He asks if you have come to stay with us now. And he says that he wishes he had wings like you."

She bent down, ruffled his hair, then reached back into the boat and gave the boy a fruit. She fanned out her wings to their full extent, and then furled then again. There was a sigh from the crowd, but she knew that there was a stiffness around her shoulders which had not been there earlier.

"I would like to stay, but my time with you is short. I will leave you soon after the sun is at his peak." She tried to rid her mouth of its dryness. "Can we go away from the river for a while? But not inside. I want to be in the air."

The king stepped forward. The common people scurried away from him.

"You are welcome here, my lady, and I would give you all the honour that is your due. I pray that you will accept this torc from me: a humble gift as token of our desire to serve."

He was holding out a band towards her, a golden version of the one that the queen wore. It looked heavy, as if it would bow down her slender neck. She did not want it, and struggled with her instinct to refuse. She was sure that the king would be offended. The crowd around were murmuring to each other, unable for the most part to comprehend the old tongue.

"I am deeply grateful, but I cannot take it with me when I leave you. I shall wear it on my arm while I am here, and return it to you when I go."

She saw Brendan give a little smile, a little nod of relief, and knew she had done right.

"I too have gifts for you." She gestured towards the boat. "These are all that is left of the beauty that was my home. I have lived with these blossoms all my days. Take them all, give them to whosoever you please. But they are not like your gold: they will fade, and their splendour will not last long."

She knew that already the blooms were less perfect than they had been. They were dwindling, curling a little at the edges as the harshness and cold of the winter air unravelled their loveliness. Quick tears pricked her eyes as she thought of the Mirror, cracked now from side to side, its shining surface crumbling like dry fungus. Feeling the sharp pains that lanced her with every breath, and the dull aching in her legs, she wondered sombrely if her own fate was close as well.

The king gestured, and some of the kitchen women ran forward. Exclamations of surprise and joy ran around the crowd as the bundles were unwrapped. The lady knew that even in this depleted state, nothing in the land could rival the magnificence of what her garden had produced.

But time was short. Clinging to Llawen's hand, she went over to the queen Gwynwi. She stood for a moment, looking at her. Her features were exactly like those she remembered from the distant past, but in other ways the two women were not alike. Long ago, she had been confident, full of maternal pride and poise. Now she was conflicted, and had an unfinished air about her. She held the lady's eyes only with difficulty.

The lady glanced back to where the king was dispensing gifts, then took the queen's arm, standing between her and Llawen.

"Come, we shall walk together. I have waited so very long for this, and now I only have a short time."

Llawen turned as if to call to his king, but the lady shook her head.

"Let him follow later if he wishes, but we will go now."

They walked through the crowd. One or two people reached out towards the lady as she passed them by, but most drew back, leaving an open path for the three to follow.

She opened her wings to arch over them, to shield them from curious gaze, and they walked in silence for a while. Before long they reached the last of the houses, and climbed a little hillock. The four grey towers of her former home were just visible over a copse of low trees, but the lady turned and looked elsewhere. There would be no going back.

Her legs wavered. Llawen supported her, his face full of anxiety.

"Are you wounded, my lady?"

She shook her head.

"Not wounded, but not well either. Time runs out for me."

"Surely not? You live forever, and our lives are like sparks in the wind beside you. How can your time run out? What will we do?"

She did not answer for a while, but leaned on his strength.

"My life is long, and yet it has been fleeting. I remember you both from when this land was very young, but it seems only a few days ago. And I change. I have not always been like this, and I do not know what I shall be next." She hesitated. "I am afraid of what may happen after we part."

They were both watching her, drinking up every word. She reached out, touched the queen's face in the way she had wanted to long ago. She gave a little sigh. She had found the mother again, yet the woman she had found was young, and she herself was the older of them. The meeting was not at all as she had imagined it would be. Gwynwi caught her hand, pressed it to her lips.

"You said I had children?"

The lady nodded.

"I saw three. But one was only an infant at your breast, and perhaps more were to follow."

"Will you grant me that prayer again? I will promise, I will do, whatever you ask." She hesitated, glanced briefly at Llawen and then gazed at the lady as though she would swallow her up. "The king grows impatient, though I swear there is no lack in me. Grant me this one thing, lady, I pray."

The lady thought back to the young couple whose pregnancy had begun outside her walls. She had wanted to believe that she had made that possible, but had never known for sure. She looked across to where the royal keep stood guard over the clustered houses.

"I do not think that is in my power to give. Not any more. Perhaps it was, once. But here and now, you must do whatever is in your own ability."

She wanted their comfort, as she felt her vitality slipping away, but the couple were too full of their own needs and anxieties. She felt a tremor run up her legs, a sharp pain in her abdomen, and despite her best intentions, the spasm must have shown in her face.

Llawen gripped her hand, and Gwynwi stepped very close to her.

"Truly, lady, you do not look well."

"I will leave you very soon. On the boat, I think. It will be best. Already I feel myself declining."

She spread out her wings once again, pushing past the stiffness in her shoulders. The bold patterning had faded to a muted series of whirls and stripes. Llawen looked very solemn, noticing how a web of fine lines was starting to wrinkle her face. Gwynwi finally overcame her hesitation and wrapped her arms around the lady in a long embrace.

"Go when you must, lady. The common people should not see you like this. Better that they think of you as ageless."

The king's voice came from behind them. The lady looked once more at Llawen and Gwynwi. She blinked back tears, and their faces blurred slightly, flowed like the river into her memories of how they had looked all those many years ago. Then she turned to greet the king as he walked up. He was wearing a large spray of her flowers at the shoulder of his cloak.

"I thank you again for your gifts, my lady. Will you come into my house now, and honour it with your presence?"

She stood there, modelling herself on the dignity she had seen Queen Gwynwi strive for.

"You are kind, sir, but my time with you is almost over. I must return to the boat, and continue my journey."

His face fell. He was like a boy still, his feelings transparent. He looked around and ran a hand through his hair.

"I wish I had known that your visit would be so fleeting. I could have spent less time distributing the gifts. More time attending to you."

She shook her head.

"No matter. I have been well cared for, and I shall remember your kingdom with pleasure. I have seen all that I wanted to see."

His features brightened once again. The lady felt Gwynwi squeeze her arm slightly, the private gesture passing between them unnoticed.

She gestured for the king to lead. They walked slowly back towards the river. Llawen's arm was steady when she might have stumbled. She was proud of herself for keeping an even pace, and not allowing the sharp pains chasing throughout her body to show in her face.

They were back at the boat. Stray petals and leaves rolled about, pushed here and there by the restless wind. But most of what she had brought was adorning the clothes and hair of the townspeople. Solemn faces and quiet whispers surrounded her.

"Would you speak with them, lady, while I stand beside you? Would you give us all your blessing? It would be an honour beyond all that we could expect."

She nodded, wondering what to say. He rushed on.

"They all think that you live in these flowers. They are saying they will look for you there after you leave us. They believe you are a visitor who has come from the world of spirits, and that you can shrink down to make your home inside the petals."

She turned to face the crowd by the riverbank, standing on the edge of the wooden staithe. She felt brittle, worn out, and old. Perhaps her years had caught up with her at last, though the Mirror had seemed to say that this was another passing stage. She had no idea what might come next, but she would not allow her doubts to show.

She spoke to them all then, knowing that most of them would not comprehend the old tongue of their own land, trusting that Brendan would tell them later, in his own way.

She thanked them for their service over the years, and for their welcome today. She praised the king and queen for the gifts they had given. And finally, not knowing when, or even if it could be fulfilled, she promised to visit them again one day. She did not really know how to deliver the blessing that the king had asked for, but she hoped that the people would receive it as such. She looked across at Brendan, wishing that she could have spent time with him as well, seeing the shared sorrow written on his face.

She walked past the line of warriors, contemplating wryly that she never had found the companion, loyal and true, that she had once imagined. She took the torc from her wrist and returned it to the king. She embraced him carefully, wary that his touch might unknowingly crush her frame. She kissed the queen, wondering if she did so as daughter or benefactress. The two women held each other for a long moment.

Then she stepped into the boat where Llawen held it steady against the current. He waited as she settled herself in the stern, then waded out with her, so she would catch the current. She put a hand on his arm, leaned in to him, and kissed him as well. His eyes were wide.

"Look after her when I am gone."

He nodded, not able to speak. Then he gave the boat one last push, and it started to drift. She looked back. Other than Llawen, the whole town was watching her from the water's edge. They looked eager, expectant.

She flinched, knowing what they wanted, and started to sing, though each breath was like a thorn in her throat. They sighed as her voice reached them over the water, diminishing as the boat was taken by the stream. Her last glimpse as she went around the next bend was of Llawen, standing waist-deep, still watching her. Then he was gone, too.

She continued singing for another two bends, letting her voice gradually fade rather than stop abruptly. Then she fell silent. The effort had been too much. The cold seeped into her skin, and she was shivering constantly. She was wilting. She knew that she would no longer be able to stand upright now, even if the boat lodged against the shore. She spread out her wings, and looked in dismay at the fragile surfaces and frayed edges. Little fragments flaked away where she inadvertently touched the sides of the boat, and she hastily furled them again. She was withering away, crumbling, just as the Mirror had done.

It was too much effort even to sit. She let herself slump over to one side as the boat bobbled along a sudden eddy. Her cheek rested on the wooden seat. A splash of colour caught her eye: one last flower, left behind by accident when the rest had been emptied. She reached out, her joints cracking in protest, and placed the blossom just in front of her.

The pale sun shone from the winter sky as she passed down the river towards the distant sea. At least she had light for her last journey, and some semblance of the warmth that she had been used to. Her eyes were becoming veiled. The world beyond the boat was fading into darkness. But the sun's rays still shone on the petals, and held her focus just a little longer.

Then her eyes closed. The flower was gone. She let herself slip away.

Richard Abbott

Transformation

THE LADY AWOKE. She felt herself floating and opened her eyes, not understanding the sensation. There was a world below her, blue and green and delightful. Down there, back on the surface, her corpse was still in the boat, still following the river. She found the vessel, found the withered body, still wrapped in its white shroud. The skin that had been hers was dried up, shrivelling, and the dead hand was still resting on the bench close to the dead flower.

The boat had already travelled a long way from her former home. It had drifted through a good fraction of the open wetlands she had once explored, and was not all that far now from where the river discharged into a wide bay. She hoped it would reach the sea, and that the carcase it carried would be tossed by waves into the deep rather than squabbled over by wild animals.

Up here, she was drifting in the emptiness she had always loved, and to which she had always returned when companionship became too intense. Recognition flared in her soul at the sensation of the void around her. She rolled, looking out at the distant stars, the strands of the golden galaxy surrounding her. This was where she belonged, and the time on the world she circled had only been a long childhood for her.

She spread her wings, stretching out the tenuous threads of energy which held the gauzy structure together. They were, she realised, even more fine than the ones she had had before. It was good: it made her complete. She wheeled, turning away from the planet, and let the solar wind propel her on.

The Mirror had placed knowledge of all this within her at some stage, along with a full remembrance of her lineage. It had lain dormant while there was no stimulus to trigger it. But she now knew who she was, and – now that she was adult – knew also that there were other star systems to visit.

She would flit like a butterfly from one to another, riding the ionised breezes that the stars breathed out. It would be slow, but she was used to the passage of years now. There would be time enough to see all those worlds.

She would fertilise the places she visited not with pollen, but with sparks of anticipation and hope. Eventually, she would meet others of her kind, dance with them, and then carry her own offspring elsewhere to lie in their stone cocoons, in their own worlds.

She would leave them to learn for themselves how to meet with others, as her species had always done. She had discovered in this world how to combine separation and companionship: so would they in theirs. It was improbable in the extreme that she would meet her own biological relatives once they had parted: so it had always been. Her time with the people near to her former home was a better preparation for maturity than anything the Mirror could have provided.

One day she would return to this particular world, and see what had become of the people she had watched. She wondered, her memory suffused with warmth, what would happen to the ones she had chosen as family. She would find out, on her next visit. They had met once, and they would meet again. They were, after all, the kindred she had adopted.

For now, it was time to move on from here. She would not stop at this world's moon. She had gazed up at it so often, and it had governed the imaginative lives of the townspeople, but it was of no interest to her now.

She would pause to inspect a number of the icy satellites further from the sun, clustered like swarming bees around their massive primaries. The Mirror had tagged a few for her, where liquid water flowed below a frozen surface. She would respect its wishes, one last time.

She tightened the mesh of her wings, feeling herself accelerate under the steady pressure of the gentle sunlight.

She was no longer in the shadows: this was the journey she was born for.

Richard Abbott

Author's Notes

In one of the tales surrounding King Arthur, we are introduced to a lady, sometimes called Elaine, whose life and death serve to expose the latent attraction between Launcelot and Guinevere. Her home is variously named as Astolat, Scalotta, or Shalott, and she is routinely associated with flowers, especially lilies. The story has been told many times in prose, verse, song, and art. Perhaps the best-known version is the poem, *The Lady of Shalott*, written by Alfred Lord Tennyson.

The several versions each highlight particular aspects of the story, and the roles of the various protagonists. The story itself can support many variations: this one goes in its own particular direction.

About the author

Richard Abbott has visited some of the places that feature in his historical fiction. To date, however, he has not had the opportunity of visiting anywhere outside the Earth that might feature in his futuristic writing.

Richard currently lives in London, England. When not writing he works on the development and testing of computer and internet applications. He enjoys spending time with family, walking and wildlife – ideally combining all three of those pursuits at the same time.

Follow the author on:

- Web site – www.kephrath.com
- Blog – richardabbott.datascenesdev.com/blog/
- Google+ – Search for "Richard Abbott"
- Facebook – Search for "Richard Abbott"
- Twitter – @MilkHoneyedLand

Look out for his other works, which include the following.

Science Fiction – full-length novels

- *Far from the Spaceports*, available from most online retailers, and general booksellers to order in

  - soft-cover – ISBN 978-0993-1684-4-4
  - ebook format – ISBN 978-0993-1684-5-1

In case of difficulty please check the website http://www.kephrath.com for purchasing options.
Feedback for this novel includes:
"...a delightful read. Abbott's characters are very personable and make for good companions as he carries us to a promising future..."

The New Podler Review of Books

"...a splendid good read... possibly the best thing the author has done to date..."

Breakfast with Pandora

- *Timing*, available from most online retailers, and general booksellers to order in

  - soft-cover – ISBN 978-0993-1684-6-8
  - ebook format – ISBN 978-0993-1684-7-5

In case of difficulty please check the website http://www.kephrath.com for purchasing options.
Feedback for this novel includes:
"...If you are looking for good science, believable personalities and suspense coupled with an immensely satisfying read then this book is for you!..."

Amazon.com reviewer

"...Mit... an ultra-smart, resourceful guy who isn't above a bit of adventure..."

Breakfast with Pandora

Historical Fiction – full-length novels

- *In a Milk and Honeyed Land*, available from most online retailers, and general booksellers to order in

  – soft-cover – ISBN 978-0993-1684-2-0

  – ebook format – ISBN 978-0993-1684-3-7

In case of difficulty please check the website http://www.kephrath.com for purchasing options. Feedback for this novel includes:
"the author is an authority on the subject, and it shows through the captivating descriptions of the ancient rituals, songs, village life, and even a battle scene... the story grabs hold of the imagination... satisfies as a love story, coming-of-age tale, and historical narrative..."

Blue Ink Review

"... The lives of these ordinary people are brought to life on the page in a way that's absorbing and credible. The changes that are going to take place in this area are quite incredible... a wonderous land that seems both alien and yet somehow familiar..."

Historical Novel Society UK Review

- *Scenes from a Life*, available from most online retailers, and general booksellers to order in

  – soft-cover – ISBN 978-0954-5535-9-3

  – kindle format – ISBN 978-0954-5535-7-9

  – epub format – ISBN 978-0954-5535-8-6

In case of difficulty please check the website http://www.kephrath.com for purchasing options. Feedback for this novel includes:

"The author is extremely knowledgeable of his subject and the minute detail brings the story vividly to life, to the point where you can almost feel the sand and the heat..."

Historical Novel Society UK Review

"...lovely description – evocative sentences or phrases that add so much to the atmosphere of the book"

The Review Group

"The striking thing about 'Scenes' is... its sensitivity: its assured, mature observation of people"

Breakfast with Pandora

- *The Flame Before Us*, available from most online retailers, and general booksellers to order in

    – soft-cover – ISBN 978-0993-1684-1-3

    – ebook format – ISBN 978-0993-1684-0-6

In case of difficulty please check the website
http://www.kephrath.com for purchasing options.
Feedback for this novel includes:
"Wide in scope and rich in detail and plot, this is an accomplished illustration of this era in the region: complex, informative, enjoyable and skilfully put together."

Historical Novel Society UK Review

"...A surprising tenderness in the face of brutality, loss, and displacement is the emotion that underpins the action..."

Breakfast with Pandora

Historical Fiction – short stories

- *The Man in the Cistern*, a short story of Kephrath, published in ebook format by Matteh Publications and available at online retailers, ISBN 978-0954-5535-1-7 (kindle) or 978-0954-5535-4-8 (epub).

- *The Lady of the Lions*, a short story of Kephrath, published in ebook format by Matteh Publications and available at online retailers, ISBN 978-0954-5535-3-1 (kindle) or 978-0954-5535-5-5 (epub).

Non-fiction

- *Triumphal Accounts in Hebrew and Egyptian*, published in ebook format by Matteh Publications and available at online retailers, ISBN 978-0954-5535-2-4 (kindle) or 978-0954-5535-6-2 (epub).

About Matteh Publications

Matteh Publications is a small publisher based in north London offering a small range of specialised books, mostly in ebook form only. For information concerning current or forthcoming titles please see
http://mattehpublications.datascenesdev.com/.